Praise for

The Downing Brothers

Sleeping with the Enemy's Daughter by Nadia Aidan is sinfully erotic...sizzling love scenes and volatile emotions... Nadia Aidan's well written plot and sultry sexual escapades made Sleeping with the Enemy's Daughter a great read.
~ *Joyfully Reviewed*

Sleeping With the Enemy's Daughter is a great read and I loved watching Camille's relationship with each brother unfold as well as watching Jacob coming to terms with his true feelings for her. I encourage everyone to go out and pick up a copy of this book ~ *Two Lips Reviews*

I0616914

THE DOWNING BROTHERS

Volume One

Sleeping with the Enemy's Daughter

A Rebound Affair

NADIA AIDAN

The Downing Brothers Volume One
ISBN # 978-0-85715-067-7
©Copyright Nadia Aidan 2010
Cover Art by Natalie Winters ©Copyright 2010
Interior text design by Claire Siemaszkiewicz
Total-E-Bound Publishing

Published in 2010 by Total-E-Bound Publishing, Think Tank, Ruston Way,
Lincoln, LN6 7FL, United Kingdom.

Manufactured in the USA.

SLEEPING WITH THE ENEMY'S DAUGHTER

Dedication

To the wonderful women of Cactus Rose

Chapter One

Camille Douglas stepped into the spacious office and slammed the door behind her with a piercing thud. At the sound of a faint noise, she whipped her head to the side to see a single picture, encased in what appeared to be an expensive gold frame, topple from the mantle and fall with a soft thump to the floor. A tiny grin tugged at the corners of her mouth, but she fought it back, even as a childish sense of triumph stole over her.

With lazy steps, she sauntered towards the centre of the room, her high heels digging into the soft plush carpet, until she came to a stop in front of a large cherry oak desk. With a slight tilt of her chin, she schooled her features into a neutral expression and bravely met the gazes of the four men that stood before her, as hostility blazed in the matching depths of their eyes.

With a quick flick of the wrist, Camille tossed her unruly curls over her shoulder and straightened her back even as droplets of sweat coated her palms. She was scared, but she had no intention of showing it. The Downing brothers had brought her there to draw blood, but she would be damned if she gave them the satisfaction of knowing that she was nervous as hell.

"I'm here as you *summoned*," she drawled in her soft, southern accent, her voice dripping with contempt.

Jacob's eyes narrowed. He was the oldest and out of all of them, he was the most arrogant. She'd attended school with him so she knew him the best, and out of all of them she hated him the most.

"You didn't have to come, although I am sure you knew it was in *your* best interests to do so," he said tightly.

She stiffened at his words, her hands balling into tight fists.

"My best interests?" Despite a valiant effort, she couldn't stop the look of scorn that she knew, without a doubt, crossed her face.

"No, Mr. Downing—" she paused to glance at each of them. "Mr. *Downings*—" she corrected. "This meeting is in no way shape or form in *my* best interests, but what choice did I really have? You offered me a way to save my family ranch, so I'm here to take it."

She stared at each of them, the bitter animosity she'd fought to mask, now blazed in her gaze as anger ignited inside her at the thought of why she was there in the first place. If it wasn't for what the ranch symbolised she would have told them all to kiss her ass a long time ago. But with the predicament she was in, she was now forced to kiss *their* asses.

The Douglas Ranch had been in her family since her great-great grandmother, Ida Douglas, a former slave with almost no education, had managed to purchase a small plot of land outside of San Antonio Texas during the Reconstruction Era. At the time, it hadn't been much, but over the years, the ranch had grown in size, eventually becoming a lucrative and extensive ranching operation, until their name was synonymous with the wealthy black elite of Texas. That had all changed six years ago when her father died and her greedy, tramp of a step-mother squandered most of the family assets in one poorly conceived business deal after the next.

By the time Camille returned from her graduate studies in Dublin six months ago, it was too late. The ranch was up for foreclosure, and everything that her family had worked so hard for was now in the hands of their bitter enemies and hated rivals — the Downings. The four Downing brothers now held her family legacy in their hands, and with the exception of going on a murderous rampage, she would stop at nothing to reclaim her family heritage.

"Have a seat, Ms. Douglas," Jackson, the second oldest said and waved his hand towards the lone chair in the middle of the room. She glanced at it. There were no other chairs in the room. She shook her head. There was no way in hell she was going to sit, while those cocky, arrogant bastards stood *over* her.

"No thank you. I'll stand."

Jackson shrugged. "Suit yourself."

Apparently, that had been their one attempt at courtesy. From the stubborn set of their matching jaw lines, Camille could tell that their southern hospitality well had probably dried up long ago — or at least it had towards her and her family. That was fine with her. She wasn't there to be courted like some dainty southern belle. She was there to hear their terms so that she could negotiate the selling of *her* property back to *her*.

"Look gentlemen. There's no sense in pretending that this is an amicable meeting, so why don't we just skip the pleasantries and get straight to business. How much is it going to cost me to get my land back?" There. She'd said it. Her heart beat frantically in her chest as she watched them glance at each other, their expressions registering surprise. She was sure her bluntness had caught them off guard. No matter. That *was* the reason why she was there so it shouldn't have come as too big of a surprise that the subject of her ranch would end up on the agenda.

Camille silently fumed, when they leaned in close to exchange hushed words. Their voices were barely more than a whisper, but she could still hear her name. She tapped her foot angrily against the soft carpeted floor, amazed by their rudeness, and a little annoyed that the sound of her stomping foot was muffled.

When they finished with their discussion, Jackson, Jeff and Jason all nodded at their older brother, as if signalling that they were in agreement.

She watched with wary eyes while Jacob studied her. His gaze settled first on her face, before leisurely drifting across her figure. A gasp of shock threatened to erupt from her lips when his eyes lingered on her overly large breasts that strained against her gray suit. As a size sixteen, it was hard to find decent clothing to contain them, but she thought she'd done a good job of hiding her chest that day. Apparently *not*. A fresh wave of fury washed over her as she bristled under his scrutiny, barely suppressing the urge to ask if he wanted a closer look when his eyes zeroed in on the area between her legs. She shook her head, appalled by his audacity. When he lingered there for several moments, she couldn't contain herself any longer.

"Mr. Downing? Is there something that you would like to *say* to me — to my face?" She snapped angrily.

Jacob arched a single eyebrow and his lips curled up into a slight grin that looked more like a leer.

Her nostrils flared at the gesture. There was nothing amusing about his actions.

"Actually, there is." His eyes held her gaze, his expression blank. "How much is the ranch worth to you?"

Camille stood there for several moments considering his question, before giving him the only answer that she could — the truth.

"It's worth everything. It's been in my family for generations, and I would do anything to keep it," she said, knowing her eyes revealed the sincerity of her words.

"Anything?"

She blinked for several seconds. There was something in his voice that gave her pause, but she finally nodded saying, "Yes. I would do *anything* to keep it." She fixed her gaze upon each of them before adding. "I cannot buy it at market value yet, but I have a trust and some money saved. I can give you some now and then work out a pay —"

"Thank you, Ms. Douglas for that offer, but we have already come to a decision on the payment plan."

Relief instantly flooded her at his words, and for the first time since she'd agreed to the meeting, she allowed the tension to seep from her body. They were going to let her buy it back. She had been so worried that with the bad blood between their families they would simply refuse to sell.

"How much? How much do I owe you?"

"It's not an amount."

She shook her head, puzzled. "I don't understand."

"It's not money we want from you."

"Then how am I supposed to pay you back for the ranch? It's worth almost three million dollars. What could I possibly give you that would compensate for the amount you paid?"

"Yourself."

Her eyes widened, not quite comprehending Jacob's statement. "Huh?"

"*You* are the payment, Camille."

His words hit her like a ton of bricks. She stared up at them, the cold expressionless masks that were their faces. A soft gasp ripped past her lips when Jacob's words finally penetrated the fog that had settled in her brain. They were serious. They wanted *her* as payment!

"P—payment how? In what capacity?" She swallowed the lump in her throat. Maybe they wanted her to be their housekeeper, because the alternative was infinitely more terrifying than the thought of scrubbing their floors and doing their dirty laundry for an eternity.

Jacob's eyes flashed with impatience.

"What do you think, Camille? *You* are the payment."

She shook her head in protest, but he ignored her.

"For six months you will serve all of our sexual needs in any way *we* see fit. You are to be available to service us at any time, and any place." She had to restrain herself from rearing back in shock when she glimpsed the tiny flash of desire in his eyes.

"If you comply with our demands for the entire time, then the ranch is yours."

She stood there stunned. Yet the shock was quickly replaced by fury.

"Absolutely not! I have a *job* gentleman and it does *not* include being your twenty-four hour mistress. Those terms are unacceptable—"

"This is not up for negotiation. This is the *only* offer we are making. You can either take it, or lose your ranch for good," Jeff said.

She whirled around to stare at Jeff, the third oldest, surprised by his boldness. But then again he *was* a Downing so what had she truly expected?

"We were under the impression that as an advice columnist and freelance writer, you work mostly from home."

She slid her gaze to Jason, the youngest, and shot angry daggers from her eyes at him for his insinuation.

A bitter chuckle escaped her lips.

"So you think because I work at home, that I having nothing but endless amounts of time to play your *mistress?*" She asked in a shrill voice.

Silence.

That's *exactly* what they thought.

Her body trembled with barely contained rage as she met their arrogant gazes. They were *insane.*

"You know what, gentleman. This has been an interesting—"

"You have two days, Camille," Jacob interrupted. "Two days to accept our offer."

Her eyes narrowed to angry slits. "And if I don't?"

"Then you forfeit any future rights to your ranch. We already own it, Camille. This is your last chance to get it back."

If she'd been closer she would have slapped him. She already *knew* they owned it—

that's why she was there in the *first* damned place.

"Two days, Camille," he repeated before nodding towards the door.

She was dismissed.

Simmering with rage, she lifted her chin higher into the air, trying to muster the last vestiges of dignity she still possessed. She spun on her heel and stomped angrily towards the door. Flinging it open with a hard bang, she moved to exit the room, but stopped instead. Twisting her head around, she fixed them each with a chilly glare.

"Fuck you. Fuck all of you," she shouted, before she slammed the door behind her.

She paused when she heard a soft thump from the other side of the door.

Ah, the sound of another expensively framed picture tumbling from the mantle. This time she didn't even *try* to hide her smile.

* * * *

Shoving her mouth full of Krispy Kreme doughnuts probably wasn't the wisest move, considering she was trying to lose weight, but she couldn't stop herself. Her meeting with the Downing brothers had sent her spiralling towards meltdown and it was either binge and pay later, or grab a gun and march back over to their ranch. She figured grabbing a doughnut would keep her out of jail, but definitely not out of Weight Watchers.

She leaned back in her kitchen chair and closed her eyes. Chewing vigorously, she savoured the sticky glaze of the sweet treat. Not for the first time she wondered what the hell the Downing brothers *really* wanted with her, because functioning as their full time mistress certainly wasn't it.

It was laughable really. They were four of the handsomest, wealthiest, and most eligible bachelors in all of Texas. Their mixed Spanish, native, and Irish heritage had proved the perfect combination for them, because they were so devastatingly handsome that it was almost nauseating. Evenly spaced two years apart with Jacob being the oldest at thirty-seven and Jason the youngest at thirty-one, the resemblance was so striking that it was impossible not to notice they were brothers.

She shoved another doughnut between her lips and moaned. As delighted as she was to binge on the over priced, high fat doughnuts, even her favourite treat couldn't distract her for very long. For the life of her, she couldn't figure out why they didn't just let her pay them for the ranch in *money*. She had money, but with the loss of her ranch she was no longer considered truly wealthy, although that's not what really mattered to her. Even after she got it back she still didn't plan to live off of the revenues any more than she had since becoming an adult. She wanted the ranch back because of what it symbolised, *not* because of the money it generated.

Shaking her head, she blew out a deep, ragged breath. She just couldn't put her finger on it. They could have any woman they wanted and yet they pretended they wanted her. It was a cruel joke, and she knew it.

At thirty-five she held no illusions regarding her limitations and failures. Her ex-husband had made sure she knew *exactly* how lacking she was. He had been cut from the same cloth as the Downings — wealthy, educated, powerful and handsome. Her father had practically forced her to marry him, even though he knew they didn't love each other. She now wished she'd had the guts to stand up to her father back then. If she had, then maybe she wouldn't have spent five years in a loveless marriage with a man who when he wasn't ridiculing her for her lack of physical beauty he was too busy screwing around on her with women who were all the things she wasn't.

It may have taken her five years to work up the nerve to leave Marcus, but she was proud that she managed to do it. If she hadn't, she would have missed out on the opportunity of a lifetime. A year after her divorce she'd been offered a fellowship to study writing at Trinity College in Dublin, and she didn't hesitate to seize the opportunity. As Jason had pointed out she *could* write her column from anywhere, and she had. She'd spent two years in Dublin splitting her time between writing her column and earning her Masters. The experience had been invaluable for so many reasons, but mainly because it offered her the chance to heal and reclaim her sense of self worth.

"And now they're trying to threaten my hard earned confidence," she gritted out between bites.

Letting out a sigh, she stood and dragged herself to the full length mirror in the hallway of the apartment she'd been forced to rent. Still dressed in her suit, she stared at her reflection. She was all right. Her russet coloured hair danced about her shoulders, and curled down to her upper back, complimenting her smooth mahogany complexion. She tilted her head to study her face more closely. Framed by long lashes, her almond shaped topaz eyes, winked back at her from above her high cheekbones which drew attention to her full lips. She'd always been described as cute, which she guessed was better than the alternative. But she was no beauty. She stepped back to look at the total package. She could stand to lose a few pounds, okay *several* pounds, but she wasn't *bad*. Still, she knew under her flattering suit, she carried pockets of fat and cellulite in more places than she wanted to contemplate.

She wondered how the perfectly made Downing brothers, with their flawless faces, and chiselled physiques would react to her less than perfect figure *and* face.

She abruptly turned from the mirror to plop back down in her chair. She couldn't care less what those arrogant assholes thought of her. *If* she decided to accept their absurd and ridiculous agreement then it would be their own damn faults if they weren't satisfied with what they got. They could have sold her the damn ranch like normal human beings!

* * * *

Jacob poured himself a shot of brandy into the glass snifter and swirled it around for several seconds before knocking it back in a single gulp. He winced as the warm liquid burned a trail down his throat to settle in his belly. Setting the glass aside, he turned from his office window and flopped down in his desk chair.

Dragging a hand across his face, he released a long breath. "What the hell did you do?" He asked himself for the hundredth time. Ever since Camille Douglas had stormed angrily from his home he'd questioned the wisdom of the ultimatum he'd issued her.

If his father were alive he'd be furious with him for putting Camille in such a compromising position. But he wasn't alive and he had Camille's mother to thank for that. Rage coursed through his veins as he curled his hands into angry fists. Every time he thought of Adel Douglas, blinding anger gripped him.

The affair between his father and Camille's mother had begun a few years after the death of his own mother. His father didn't think anyone knew, neither one of them did, but everyone in all of Macon knew. Adel's affair with his father stretched on for years, until it was no longer a secret to anyone.

Naturally, Adel's husband, Earl, developed a burning hatred towards his father and the entire Downing clan, which became the source of the bitter feud between the two families, a feud that turned particularly nasty after the death of Adel. Jacob was certain that the stress from learning of Adel's betrayal after her death, along with the cutthroat tactics of Earl Douglas to undermine his ranching business, had killed his father. Camille's parents ruined his entire life, and his father had died because Adel betrayed him and broke his heart.

Over the years, his brothers had moved on, entertaining the possibility that maybe Adel was innocent, but Jacob didn't believe that for one second, which was why he'd devoted the last two years of his life to acquiring the fledging Douglas ranch. He only wished Earl Douglas was still alive to see that despite all of his lying, scheming and cheating, he could no more keep his ranch out of the hands of the Downings, than he could keep his wife.

Jacob relished the thought that his precious daughter would soon be added to the list. If the old man had been alive he would have surely died had he learned of the proposition he'd issued to Camille.

A wry smile crossed his face at that thought as he stood and poured himself another glass of brandy. This time he sipped on it slowly as his thoughts drifted from Earl Douglas to his daughter.

"Ahhh, yes, the lovely, untouchable, perfect Camille," he murmured sarcastically as he glowered at the glass he held in his hand.

He'd known Camille all his life, but always from a distance. They'd attended the same schools, lived in the same social circle, even shared some of the same friends, but their contact with each other had always been limited. Jacob suspected because her father feared that his family would use her as a pawn to manipulate him. He was sure she'd been warned repeatedly to stay away from those *evil* Downing brothers. No matter what her father had said, she had certainly listened. When she wasn't avoiding him entirely, she'd always treated him with cool distain. He'd always gotten the distinct impression that she thought he was beneath her.

He chuckled bitterly. Her blood probably ran cold at the thought of having to sleep with a Downing, as if she would sully herself by the very act. Despite a valiant attempt not to let his thoughts stray in that direction, an image of Camille entwined in his arms, her lush nude body glistening with a sheen of sweat, unwittingly popped into his head, causing a low groan to escape his lips. His mood soured as he downed the rest of his brandy. He was attracted to her. He'd been fighting it ever since she'd come back to Macon, but it was hard to ignore that the rail thin girl he'd remembered had blossomed into a beautiful, voluptuous woman.

"Life father, like son," he muttered dryly. What was it about the Douglas women that drew men — Downing men especially.

Before she'd returned he'd had no plans to sell her ranch to *anyone*. He'd taken the Douglas land. He'd gotten his revenge. Then he'd caught a glimpse of her one evening while he was in town purchasing supplies for the ranch, and in that moment everything had changed. The feud wasn't over. He wouldn't be satisfied until he took everything from the Douglas family — including their virtuous daughter — *especially* their daughter.

His brothers thought he was crazy. Hell if he were them, he would too. But then Camille had walked into his office that morning and they'd all stood at attention. They'd practically fallen over themselves to agree to his plan. He couldn't blame them. She was alluring with her feathery soft glossy curls and rich, silken skin that was as smooth and flawless as a dark chocolate dessert.

However, now that he had time to mull over his proposition, he realised it nagged at him that he'd included them in the first place. She was just supposed to be a means to an end — a tool for revenge. So why did the thought of sharing her with his brothers rankle him? He knew why. Because he wasn't good at sharing. Not women — not anything.

He dragged a hand down his face and leaned back in his chair, now furious with himself that he'd set in motion a chain of events he was now powerless to stop. What had seemed like a perfect plot for revenge was slowly starting to feel like a huge mistake.

Chapter Two

Camille fidgeted nervously in her car as she released a long, deep breath and gripped the steering wheel until her knuckles turned red. Glancing towards the house, she fixated on the light shining from the second floor. She gulped deeply. It was foolish to hope they weren't home, or that they had all gone to sleep.

She now had—she glanced at her watch—*less* than thirty minutes to march inside and begin her contractual *obligation* to them.

Her decision had not been an easy one. She'd spent a sleepless night and a restless day pondering their offer. There were few—correction—there were *no* other options. This was her last chance—they knew it and so did she. Now the question was whether her family ranch was worth the humiliation of being at the beck and call of four men that she'd been taught to despise since the day she could say the word *Downing*.

Reaching for her purse, she dragged in a deep breath and piled out of her sporty Mercedes Coup—one of the last testaments to her life *before* her greedy, stupid stepmother had made such luxuries, just that *a luxury.* Now the bitch was long gone, off to find herself yet another rich widower, while she was there trying to pick up the pieces. It wasn't fair.

With jerky movements, she ambled towards the front door and pressed the doorbell. How many times she'd screamed aloud and silently that it wasn't fair, she couldn't recall, but what she did know was that no matter how many times she said it, the end result was still the same. No, it wasn't fair, but then life never was.

Camille's heart skipped a beat when the door swung open. She swallowed the lump in her throat when her eyes met the steely blue gaze of none other than Jacob Downing. He stepped aside, and ushered her in.

With a soft thud, the heels from her shoes dug into the welcome rug that covered the doorstep. Not quite ready to face Jacob, she let her eyes dart about the foyer area. The last time she was there she'd entered from a different way, apparently because it was closer to their office. Now in the main entrance, she could see more of the actual home and from what she saw of it she had to admit it was nice. It was a classic ranch design but the décor was contemporary, with its russet stucco walls and its imported Schonbek chandeliers of the finest hand cut Swarovski crystal. It was definitely a man's home, but it was clear that that man had expensive tastes.

"Come along," Jacob murmured as he placed his large hand against the small of her back and urged her forward. "This way," he said when she hesitated.

She nodded curtly before she forced herself to plant one foot in front of the other in order to ascend the stairs. Her hand trembled slightly and she gripped the banister tighter to steady herself.

Her nervousness increased steadily as they meandered their way through the home. Like her own family ranch home, this one was huge, and they walked for several seconds through winding corridors, before they stopped at a door.

Jacob dug into his pocket and pulled out a small key before slipping it into the lock and turning the knob.

He stepped aside to let her walk through the doorway first.

As soon as she stepped inside, she stopped in her tracks.

"This apartment has four bedrooms, two baths and a full kitchen. You can enter and exit from the garage which is through that door," he said as he gestured towards a door adjacent to the kitchen area.

"It's very private. My brothers and I will leave it up to you to decide whether you want housekeeping to come in and clean—"

She spun around to face him. "But I already have an apartment."

His lips twisted into a disapproving frown. "Did we not make it clear to you that you are to be *available* to us at *any* time?"

She gritted her teeth together fighting against the tiny voice in her head that screamed at her to rake her nails down his face.

"This apartment is for *our* convenience. Not yours."

She stood there fuming, but didn't argue. What was there to say, really? She'd already agreed to this stupid charade. She knew the terms. If she was having a hard time accepting them then that was *her* problem not theirs.

"Do all four of you live here?"

He nodded. "I have a condo in Dallas because I do a lot of business there. Jackson also has a house in Houston, but basically this is our home."

Her head began to spin at the revelation. *Omigod.* With nothing but a few steps separating her from them, she could very well find herself *servicing* them more than she did anything else.

"If you give me your keys I will have movers transfer your things here. We'll also take care of breaking the lease on your apartment—"

She opened her mouth to protest.

"You won't need it," he added.

Her lips pursed into a frown, although she knew he was right. She tensed when he stepped towards her, his large frame edging into her personal space. She immediately took a step back, but his hand shot out to grasp her wrist, halting her futile attempt to escape his looming presence.

With hooded eyes, he leisurely studied her face. "When was the last time you took a lover?" he asked, his deep voice sliding over her with that husky quality that out of all of them, was unique to him.

"Excuse me?"

His eyes darkened with irritation. "When was the last time you had sex, Camille?"

Her mouth fell open in shock. "That's none of your business! What I did before has—"

"Do I need to remind you that fighting me at *every* turn is not something I consider satisfying *or* pleasing?"

"So besides being your *mistress on a string*, I now can't speak my mind or have *any* opinion?"

His eyebrows lifted at her outburst, before they snapped back down to frame unyielding eyes. "Not when it comes to sex. So *again*, when was the last time?"

Her nostrils flared at his words. She turned away from him then, effectively wrenching her wrist from his grasp. She was so embarrassed. How could she admit that she hadn't slept with a man in over *three* years? Her ex-husband had stopped even pretending to desire her a year before the divorce and while in Dublin she was too busy trying to reclaim the person that she once was that she didn't even consider opening herself up to a relationship. She ducked her head when her face began to flush with heat.

"Th—three years," she whispered, unable to meet his penetrating gaze.

"That probably means you don't have very many pieces of lingerie," he mumbled more to himself than to her, apparently unfazed by her humiliating declaration.

"I'll go shopping with you tomorrow. My brothers and I don't have *exact* tastes but they are similar. They can take you out later if they don't like my selections."

Her gaze snapped to his face. "So you make a habit of sharing women?"

He shrugged. "The younger three do, *sometimes*—"

"But you don't?" She asked, wondering why that was.

"Nope. This is my first time." His eyes seemed to burn a hole through her clothing as they travelled the length of her figure, much like he'd done two days ago in his office. "I'm possessive by nature," he said softly.

Camille's eyes grew wide at his statement, wondering exactly what he meant by that. She got the distinct impression that *all* of them were possessive by nature.

She opened her mouth to ask him to explain when a soft knock sounded at the door. Moments later it swung open.

Her heart squeezed tightly in her chest when she saw Jason, Jeff and Jackson stride through the doorway.

Damn.

She'd thought she'd at least have the first night off, but apparently not.

* * * *

Camille glanced at Jacob when he nodded at them.

They all returned his nod, before smiles broke out across their faces. She studied them as some type of silent communication passed between all four of them. She started to ask what was going on when Jacob spoke.

"She hasn't had sex in three years," he said casually.

She closed her eyes as waves of embarrassment washed over her.

"Really? Why not?" Jackson asked, turning his gaze towards her.

Her stomach dropped. She didn't know how to answer that. She wondered if they didn't really care if she answered, but when they all stood there silently waiting with expectant eyes she figured they cared after all.

"I—I um went through a divorce. And then I moved to Ireland. And I—I needed to get over my divorce," she stammered.

"You still love him?"

She shook her head at Jackson.

"No," she answered simply, relieved when they dropped the subject, seemingly satisfied with her answer.

"Take off your clothes."

She stared at Jacob. "Huh?"

She nodded dumbly when impatience flashed in his eyes. *Okay, I can see how my questions could get annoying.*

Reaching for the hem of her sweater, she pulled it over her head and tossed it aside, before unfastening her jeans and shucking them down her thighs. She was so mortified when she had to hop slightly just to get them off because they were too tight.

"*All* of your clothes," Jacob whispered.

Her stomach clenched into tiny knots when she lifted her gaze to stare at each of them. There had only been three lovers in her entire life, and none of them had ever been particularly overjoyed when they saw her naked. She had *finally* reclaimed her self esteem− −she couldn't backslide now, and she knew the Downing brothers had nothing but revenge on their minds. They would make her strip naked and then burst into fits of laughter. She was certain of it, and she refused to be a malicious pawn in their game. She'd agreed to their absurd bargain, but she refused to be ridiculed by them.

She jerked her head towards the light switch. "Can we dim the lights?"

"No," Jacob said firmly.

She pursed her lips into a frown at his refusal. She glanced around at all of them, her eyes pleading. What she saw in their gazes confused her. There was some impatience, which she figured was due to her stalling, but that was overwhelmed by the sparks of desire that churned in the depths of their eyes.

Their desire was encouraging, but it wasn't enough. She lowered her head, as tears burned the backs of her eyes. She couldn't do it.

She'd never had the courage to undress with the lights on. She didn't know how to do it now and certainly not with all of them standing there. They were just *so* perfect, and she was just so *not*.

She stiffened when Jacob stepped in front of her and reached around her back to unfasten her bra.

Leaning down, he placed a slow wet trail of soft kisses against her neck as he gingerly pried her lacy undergarment from her body.

"Don't." Jacob commanded when she moved to lift her hands to cover her breasts.

She stopped.

In a heartbeat he dragged her into his embrace and lowered his head to seize her mouth in a deep, hungry kiss. His tongue slipped between her lips, stroking inside her mouth, lighting a fire that made her nipples harden and her pussy ache.

Tearing his lips from hers he slid down her body. With slow, torturous movements he placed gentle kisses across her jaw, down the column of her throat, between her breasts, and against her stomach. Once on his knees, he lifted his hands to loop his fingers under the elastic of her underwear.

"Look at me," he barked out when she slid her gaze to the floor. She shifted her eyes to meet his. She held his gaze as he slowly pushed her panties past her hips, over her ass and down her legs. She stepped out of them, shocked when instead of flinging them aside, he balled them up and slipped them into his pocket.

"You won't need them," he murmured softly. "While you are inside these walls, you will not wear *any* panties," he said and leaned forward to place gentle kisses against the mound of her pussy.

She cried out when he slipped his tongue between the folds of her wet heat, his warm breath tickling the sensitive skin of her shaved pussy. He stroked his tongue back and forth, ploughing though her moist flesh, dragging ragged cries from her lips.

"Mmmm. You taste so good. I can't wait to fuck your pussy," he groaned before he shifted back on his heels and stood up.

He glanced over his shoulder at his brothers.

She'd been so focused on Jacob that she'd forgotten all about them.

They walked forward, their eyes now glowing with blatant lust. She looked down, shocked to see the soft cotton of their sweat pants tenting where their large erections poked out.

Jacob ushered her into the living room. There was a large dark oak table in the centre of the room, with soft, mauve cushions covering it. It was an odd table, but she thought nothing of it. She moved to sit down on a nearby couch, not knowing what else to do, but Jacob halted her in midstride when he wrapped his arm around her waist.

She stood there trembling with anticipation while each of them stripped out of their clothing. She worked hard to stifle the combined gasp of shock and moan of pleasure. As she'd known, they were all perfection. Broad chests, defined abs, taut muscular legs. Everywhere she looked, stood chiselled perfection and large, thick cocks. She gulped deeply. She knew she must have looked like a deer caught in the headlights but in truth that was exactly how she felt.

Her heart stopped when Jacob reached into a small drawer beside the couch and pulled out condoms and *lubrication?* She gasped. Jacob shot her a curious look but said nothing of her shocked gasp or wide eyes. Placing the items aside, she stood there dumbly while he directed the others. She knew he was giving them their positions, which was completely surreal to her. She thought they would take their turns with her, or something. She really hadn't prepared herself for the possibility that she would be fucked simultaneously by four men in their prime. If this was what her nights were going to be like for the next six months, there was no way in *hell* she was going to last. Physically, she just wouldn't be able to keep up.

"Hop on the table Camille," Jacob instructed.

She glanced back at the table for the first time realising *why* it had cushions on it. In the back of her mind she wondered if they had bought the table that way or had it cushioned after they realised the utility in doing so.

With all the gracefulness of a bull in a china shop, she dragged herself on top of the table.

Jackson followed behind her.

"Lie down and open your legs," he whispered.

She was getting the hang of this. They would command and then she would do.

Leaning back, she lifted her knees and spread her thighs.

She watched with anticipation as Jackson settled himself between her thighs. Leaning forward he buried his face in her pussy.

"Oh," she cried out on a strangled moan when he began to fuck her with his mouth, alternating between shoving his tongue in and out of her hole and nibbling on her clit.

When he took two fingers and plunged them inside of her she nearly flew off the table.

"Oh, God," she moaned as Jackson stroked his fingers inside of her, his lips sucking her clit hard.

It had been so long since a man had pleasured her and she could feel her orgasm quickly building at the centre of her pussy.

Her legs began to tremble with the force of her nearing climax. Clenching her eyes shut, she threw her head back, her spine arching as she came.

"Jackson," she screamed, her hands flying to his hair, her fingers digging into his scalp as she pumped her hips off the table to grind her pussy against his face.

When the final aftershocks of her climax shuddered through her, she relaxed back against the table, spent.

But rest was to elude her that night.

Still thoroughly satiated, she felt Jackson lift her for a second, before he settled beneath her. The thickly muscled plane of his torso brushed against her back as she stretched out above him.

His cock nudged between the folds of her ass and she sucked in a breath. She had never been fucked in the ass before, and she was both thrilled and terrified by the idea. All thoughts of terror were quickly shoved from her mind when Jackson scooted them both towards the end of the table, so that if she tipped her head back it would rest just against the edge of the table.

She was curious about how this position was going to work when Jeff hopped up on the table to straddle her stomach.

She moaned when he leaned over to take her breasts into his hands. He massaged her breasts in his hands, playing with their lush softness for several moments. Then with gentle but firm strokes, he tugged at her nipples. A loud hiss escaped her lips when he leaned forward to feast upon them.

"Jeff," she cried out when he buried his face into her chest.

For several moments he kneaded her breasts in his large hands, before squashing them together so that he could flick his tongue across the stiffened peaks of her nipples.

Her pussy began to quiver again as the tingling sensations slid from her sensitive nipples, down her spine to the centre of her moist heat. A strangled moan erupted from her mouth when he lifted his head from her breasts, and moved up her body to completely straddle her chest.

She lifted her head from the end of the table to watch what Jeff was doing, although she could feel every wondrous sensation.

He reached for lube from somewhere behind him and dribbled the cool liquid across her breasts.

She hissed softly as shivers racked her body when he massaged the slippery wetness into her breasts moments before he slid his cock between the full mounds.

"Ohhhh," she cried out and her head fell back when Jeff began to vigorously fuck her breasts.

With her head back and her mouth open, Jason seized the opportunity to press his stiff cock against her parted lips. It was in that moment when she finally understood why Jackson had positioned her in such a manner. *Everyone* now had access.

She hesitated briefly before she stuck out her tongue to swipe across the head of his dick.

"Shit," he hissed as he clenched his jaw tight. "Suck it," he commanded softly.

Their eyes met as she opened her mouth at the same moment Jason pressed his cock between her lips.

He groaned loudly, his hand gripping her face on both sides.

She wrapped her lips securely around his cock and sucked hard, taking him deep into her mouth letting the tip of his cock graze the back of her throat.

With the position she was in, he had to stroke his cock in and out of her mouth as she was powerless to set the rhythm while she worked furiously at sucking his hard length.

"Ah, Camille," Jason rasped, his slow strokes growing more urgent, though he was still careful not to thrust too hard into her mouth given the vulnerable position.

Her tongue swirled around the thick base of his dick when he entered and then slid across the slit in the middle of the head when he pulled out. His breath came in short pants every time she flicked her tongue around the crown of his cock, before dipping under the sensitive fold of skin. His eyelids slid shut as his head fell back — the veins in his neck bulging against his skin.

She continued to suck his dick as he stroked slowly in and out of her mouth until suddenly she felt pressure against her anus.

She tensed, which caused Jason to break his rhythm but he didn't stop, and neither did Jeff as he quickened his thrusts between the valley of her breasts.

She stiffened when Jackson reached down between their bodies to stroke one lubricated finger inside her ass, pushing through the clenching muscles. He stroked his finger in and out of her virgin anus before he added another lubricated finger.

"Relax," crooned Jackson.

She couldn't. The pressure was overwhelming.

"Close your eyes and focus on the heat building inside your pussy," whispered Jackson.

She did — and it helped. The pressure was still there, but it was different. She could feel her pussy beginning to clench and unclench with the new sensation of having her rectum probed.

"Jackson," she cried out in distress when he replaced his plunging fingers with the head of his cock.

"It's alright Camille. Just relax." She heard Jacob say in the distance.

At his words, some of the tension flowed from her body. She didn't know why, but when he said it, she believed it.

She clenched her eyes tight as Jackson fed his condom lubricated cock into her anus, inch by inch. The coolness of the lubricating gel made her tense up again.

"Camille, baby, it's okay. You have to relax," Jacob whispered again.

Her eyes flew open then when at the same time Jackson plunged the last inch of his cock inside her rectum, Jacob surged forward to bury his dick deep inside her dripping cunt. She'd been so fixated on Jackson's entry that she never noticed Jacob sliding along the length of her body to grip her thighs and spread them apart.

It was all just too much. The sensations were overwhelming as each brother probed her body with their massive cocks.

Her pussy began to vibrate with another orgasm as Jacob pounded inside her, his cock hammering into her tight sheath over and over again.

"God, Camille, you're so tight," Jacob rasped out. She knew it was him. Surprisingly, she already knew the distinct, timber of each of their deep voices, but Jacob's gravelly tone was easy to distinguish.

Loud grunts and rough groans filled up the spacious room, echoing against the walls. She laid there, the centre of their lusts while they both used and pleasured her body at the same time.

Jason was the first to lose control.

She could tell he was close to coming when his strokes grew more haphazard, his hips jerking wildly back and forth.

She released a soft moan, letting the vibrations glide across his cock as she tightened her lips around him.

"I'm coming," he rasped out moments before his cock exploded, shooting jet after jet of warm, milky semen into her mouth.

Mindful, of the position she was in, Jason immediately pulled his still rigid length out of her mouth and lifted her head so that she could swallow his cum down her throat without choking.

Still holding her head, he leaned down to press a soft kiss against her lips before he stepped away from her, disappearing from her line of vision.

She was so intent upon searching for Jason that it took her several moments to realise that Jacob, Jeff and Jackson had all stopped to shift her body down so that her head could rest fully on the table.

As soon as she was fully on the table, they resumed fucking her with deep, hard strokes.

Jacob was the roughest, as he slammed into her clenching sheath with penetrating thrusts.

She could hear guttural sounds coming from his mouth as he fucked her, his words unintelligible.

As he held her thighs wide, all she could do was lose herself in the sensation of having him ram his huge erection into her cunt, the tip of his dick brushing against her G-spot, causing white hot shocks to surge through her body with each brutal stroke.

Abruptly, she felt Jeff stiffen above her, moments before a shower of tiny beads of warmth tickled her breasts and nipples.

She lifted her head to see Jeff's head roll back on stiff shoulders that bunched and corded with tension, as he grasped his cock in his hand, wringing out the last drops of his semen. She stuck out her tongue just in time to catch the final tiny droplets of his cum that splattered all the way to her lips.

The action drew Jeff's gaze, and a crooked grin lifted his mouth before he leaned forward to place a gentle peck against her forehead.

With achingly slow movements he slid from her body and off the table.

Much like she did with Jason she tried to watch where he disappeared to, but just like the last time her attention was dragged back to the thrusting cocks of the two men that remained inside her body.

"Oh!" Her eyes widened as Jackson and Jacob flipped her. She was amazed at the ease with which they did it. The effort seemed well coordinated since neither one pulled out to do it. She wondered just how many times they had fucked the same woman at the same time, but then remembered Jacob had said this was his first time at sharing.

From the new position, Jackson was able to work his dick deeper inside her. Shoving his cock forward, be buried his stiff erection deep into her rectum over and over again with vigorous strokes.

"Jackson," she cried out. Her anus was burning and though she could feel tiny waves of pleasure, it did nothing to mask the twinge of pain that accompanied every thrust into her ass.

With deep probing strokes, he pounded into her, his balls slapping against her flesh.

At the same time, Jacob surged his hips upwards, sinking his cock into her dripping pussy.

"Yes, Camille. Yes," she heard Jackson roar out just as his body stiffened and warm cum burst from his cock to fill up the condom that separated their bodies.

He leaned forward, his warm breath sliding across her shoulder as his cock twitched deep inside her anus, still pumping seed into the thin barrier of the condom.

"Mmmm," he moaned out deeply before he placed a gentle kiss against the back of her neck and slipped his cock from her body.

"Ahhh," she cried out softly, the withdrawal of his erection causing tiny slivers of pleasure-pain to crawl up her spine.

Another sharp cry escaped from her lips when Jacob pushed her back so that she could straddle him fully, his huge cock now buried to the hilt inside her cunt. Her chest heaved from exertion. She wasn't to get even a moment's break!

"Ride me," he whispered, and his hands gripped her hips, his nails digging into the soft flesh.

She lifted her hips to ride him, but he didn't really give control over to her. Clutching her waist, he jerked her down on his cock, impaling her hard on his shaft.

"Jacob," she screamed throwing her head back, her hair brushing against her shoulders.

"That's it baby. Ride my cock."

Her breasts jiggled wildly as he forced her down on his dick, ploughing his stiff erection through the tight muscles and tender flesh of her pussy.

Her cunt was so wet from all of the sensations of being fucked by him and his brothers that her juices dribbled all over his bare cock.

With Jacob's rough stabbing strokes up into her pussy and his steel length scraping against her clit with each thrust, she could feel another orgasm approaching.

"I'm coming. I'm coming," she rasped out. Her body trembled and her channel pulsed around Jacob's pounding length. Clenching her eyes shut, she stiffened above him as her climax roared through her body like a raging fire. Pumping her hips wildly, she bounced on his cock as she came in a blinding rush that was so powerful it sent her hurling forward against his chest.

Lying spent against Jacob's torso, she panted while he reached around to cup the full globes of her ass. Clutching her ass, he jerked her down on his cock at the same time he rammed his dick up inside her. He pounded into her still spasming pussy so hard, that the sounds of his flesh slapping against hers echoed off the walls. Holding her tight, he impaled her on his shaft with deep, stabbing strokes before he suddenly jerked beneath her.

"Shit, Camille," he growled, his warm breath tickling her ear.

With his eyes clenched shut and his muscles corded tight, he released a loud roar as he dug his fingers deep into her ass.

She worked her inner muscles, clenching and unclenching her pussy around his cock.

"Camille," he growled out on a strangled groan just as she felt his dick jerk inside of her and erupt, spurting loads of hot cum deep into her cunt.

He came for a long time, his cock shooting endless jets of cum into her pussy until some spilled from her hole.

She remained still against his chest, limp as a rag doll, while he panted beneath her. Exhausted and thoroughly satiated, she closed her eyes then and drifted off to sleep with Jacob's cock still nestled deep inside her tender sheath.

* * * *

Jacob lifted a sleeping Camille off of him for just a moment to hop down from the table and gather her into his arms before padding on bare feet to her bedroom where he gently laid her on the bed, and tucked her under the covers. He stood there watching her as he experienced a moment's hesitation before he shucked aside his reservations and slipped under the covers beside her.

His eyes widened in surprise when she instantly rolled over into his arms. He lifted a shaky hand to push back a curly tendril of hair from her forehead as he held her against him. *What was he doing?* As soon as he tucked her into bed he should have gotten up and left, just as his brothers had done. But here he lay, wide awake with Camille snuggled in his arms.

He released a long sigh and let his eyes drift closed, although he knew sleep would elude him that night. Too many disturbing thoughts brewed inside his head to allow his mind to settle into slumber.

For starters, he felt like an ass. For some reason, he'd never considered that there was a softer, vulnerable side to Camille. When they were younger, she'd always come across as confident, possessed of a quiet dignity. And when he saw her again, weeks ago, and the beautiful woman she'd grown into, he'd been sure that she still possessed that same confidence. How could she not? She was a wealthy, beautiful woman. Who wouldn't fall at her feet to do her bidding? And then he'd glimpsed the fiery spirit inside her when she'd stormed in and out of his office days ago like a summer hurricane, but tonight she'd shown him another side of herself. A side he'd never seen before.

He'd almost called the entire thing off when he watched moisture gather in her eyes as she protested removing her clothing before them. She was a beautiful, sensual woman. He'd never suspected she was insecure when it came to her body. Her figure was lush and feminine, just the way he liked his women. He loved how her soft thighs had cushioned him as he rode her and that her round hips had been supple as he held her above him while she bounced up and down on his cock. She had no reason to be ashamed of her body, and yet he'd seen it on her face, and in that moment he'd cursed himself for putting that look of fear in her eyes. She was vulnerable and that knowledge both surprised and pleased him. Dumb as he was, he'd placed Camille on a pedestal of sorts. In his eyes, she was the haughty and conceited Douglas girl. For so long that's what she'd been to him that he'd allowed himself to forget that she was a woman, who had her insecurities just like any other woman. It was easy to hate her when she was just his enemy's daughter, but to see her as Camille the woman, made it harder to hold onto his anger towards her.

She mumbled softly and snuggled deeper into his embrace, and he stroked his fingers up and down the bare skin of her shoulder, holding her close. He ached to roll her beneath him and ride her lush body again, but he did his best to tamp down his growing arousal. She'd had a long day. This was a huge adjustment for her and he knew she needed to rest. Besides, he didn't quite trust himself at the moment with his lack of control.

As part of the contract, they'd all verified their sexual health with their medical records and agreed to use protection at all times. Although Camille was on birth control, they'd just felt it was simply in all of their best interests to use condoms as well. He'd insisted on that point and then agreed to it, but when he'd settled between her warm thighs all thoughts of that one stipulation had flown from his head.

He hadn't forgotten to use protection with a woman since his early days in college. He dragged in a deep breath. *How the hell did you forget to use a condom, you jackass?* It just didn't make sense to him, given his pragmatic diligence when it came to these things. And yet, he didn't even think about using one until the moment he felt himself exploding deep within her, but by then it had been too late. His lack of control and complete loss of willpower almost shocked him more than what he'd actually done.

She suddenly shifted against him to toss her leg over his. He stiffened when her thigh brushed against his hardening length, causing his erection to poke out against the white sheet. In that moment he knew he should have done what any gentleman would do. Drag himself out of her bed, and run to the nearest cold shower. But he was no gentleman, and yet at the same time he would like to think he wasn't a complete jerk either.

So while he suffered most of the night in a painfully aroused state, he kept his small promise to himself and did not make love to her again that night.

Chapter Three

Jacob sat on the couch in the family sitting room with the television channel tuned to ESPN. The screen might as well have been blank, and the sound on mute, for all the attention he paid the programme.

Jason was visiting with Camille at the moment, and while the thought of his brother making love to her still left him unsettled, the sight of them upstairs laughing together was even more disturbing.

Driven by some compulsion to see her for a third time that day, he'd entered her apartment and had been shocked to see her and Jason sitting at her kitchen table playing Scrabble. *Scrabble?* He should have been happy he hadn't walked in on them making love, but he wasn't happy at all.

Over the past few months of their arrangement she'd opened up to his brothers. Somehow in the short time, they'd gone past the point of being just lovers and now seemed as if they were fast becoming *friends*. That is everyone except him.

When he and Camille weren't making love, their time together was awkward and tense. He knew he was partially to blame. Unlike his brothers, he just didn't put the kind of effort they did into getting to know her, although it wasn't because he didn't want to. He'd seen her with his brothers, how she interacted with them. She was different around them. He didn't make the effort to get to know her because when she was with *him* she put up a wall between them. He frowned at that thought. Why the hell was he the only one she kept at arm's length?

"What are you mad about now?"

He'd been so deep in thought that he hadn't heard anyone come in. He dragged his gaze to Jackson's face as his brother strolled into the room to plop himself down on the other end of the couch.

"Who says I'm mad?"

Jackson grinned. "That sour look on your face kind of clued me in." He leaned back against the couch and folded his arms across his broad chest. "So, what's up?"

He shrugged. "I don't know. Nothing really," he lied.

Jackson arched a single eyebrow and studied him.

Jacob frowned under the weight of his brother's intense scrutiny. "What?" he finally snapped unable to take the silence any longer.

Jackson curled his lips into a small grin. "I think your woman upstairs is to blame for your bad mood."

"She's not my woman."

"But you want her to be."

He glared at his younger brother, and opened his mouth to protest, but Jackson didn't let him get a word out.

"Why don't you spend more time trying to get to know her?"

He scrunched his face up into a frown. "Because she doesn't want me to get to know her."

"That's not true and you know it. I just think it's hard for her to let her guard down with you. You still blame her family for dad's death and she knows it. I imagine it's hard for her to trust you."

"Did she say that?"

"Not in so many words."

But she *had* said something to the effect, which proved his point. She had no interest in getting to know him better. He shoved a hand through his hair as a sigh escaped his lips.

"It's hard for me to just let go of the past, Jackson. Her parents, each in their own way, destroyed dad. I don't think I can ever forgive them for that."

Jackson stood to his feet, placed a reassuring hand on his shoulder and squeezed lightly.

"No one's asking you to forgive *them*, but it's not fair to Camille that you continue to hold her responsible for her parents' mistakes."

His gaze shot to his brother's face. "So you want me to terminate the contract then?"

Jackson's eyes twinkled with mischief. "Hell, no. We're all having way too much fun, Camille included. I just want you to *try* to put aside all of that bitterness you carry inside of you long enough to get to know her better. I know you want to," he said softly before he quietly slipped out of the room.

He grimaced at Jackson's departing back. His brother was right, but Jackson just didn't understand. As the oldest, he'd been the one to shoulder the burden of raising his brothers after their father's heart attack. He'd wanted to go away to college to become an attorney, not attend the local university and take over his family business, and the raising of his teenage brothers, but at eighteen he'd done it.

As Jackson had so bluntly pointed out, he was attracted to Camille and wanted to peel away her layers to reveal the woman that his brothers were starting to see, but it was difficult to unlearn years of bitterness and resentment. No, Camille wasn't responsible, nor was she to blame for her parents' mistakes. Yet it was as if a tug of war raged inside him. He wanted to hate her for what she represented, but he couldn't.

He released a ragged breath, stood and clicked off the television. Tonight he would get some sleep—alone. He didn't need to wander back to Camille's bed right now, not with all the conflicting thoughts swirling around in his head. As he stalked off to his bedroom, he promised himself that he would at least try to take Jackson's words to heart. He would be the first to extend the olive branch.

* * * *

Camille was typing away on her computer trying to get her column in by her deadline when she heard the key rattle in the lock, before the door swung open.

They were insatiable—*all* of them! Not a day went by without one or all four of them visiting her. She rarely slept alone at night, and now her days were filled with random visits such as this one.

At first, she had been just as hesitant and wary of them as they were of her. The feud between their families was so ingrained in them that it was hard to let down their guards. Yet somehow in the past three months she'd managed to establish a tenuous truce with all of them—no take that back—all of them, except Jacob. Like the rest of them, he visited her regularly but where Jason loved to play board games, Jeff enjoyed watching football with her, and Jackson liked to simply talk about any and everything, Jacob remained sullen and distant. Yet when they made love, there was always something there, something lingering in the air between them that demanded acknowledgement but both of them refused to give voice to it.

Thoughts of Jacob always gave her a headache. He was an enigma and the longer she spent trying to figure him out the less she actually could. Sighing, she closed her laptop and stood to greet whoever had just entered.

She turned the corner from her living room to come face to face with the very object of her thoughts. He looked wild eyed and confused, as if he didn't quite realise what had driven him to seek her company. That was the look she saw often on his face when he visited her.

"Are you busy?"

She jerked her head over her shoulder, in the direction of her office. "I have a deadline for my column. I'm just working on getting it done."

"Are you going to work on it all weekend?"

She shook her head. "No. I was almost done actually." She lifted her brows. "Why?"

A wary grin crossed his face, causing tiny butterflies to beat against her stomach. They were all equally handsome, but only Jacob could make her melt with just one look, one smile, one caress. She shook her head trying to push the destructive thoughts from her mind. Out of all the brothers, she *had* to be attracted to the one who hated her the most. She'd never figured herself to be a masochist, but if this didn't have *love to be hurt* written all over it then she didn't know what did.

"I wanted to see if you were free for dinner tonight," he said casually.

She struggled to keep her features neutral as she searched his face, trying to read any deception in his eyes. She saw none. Yet she was still wary. At any moment she expected Jacob to reveal *why* he'd really brought her there and his true plan for revenge. She still didn't completely trust the rest of them, but she definitely didn't trust Jacob. He had only shown her coldness. His offer of dinner raised her suspicions.

She folded her arms across her chest. "You don't have to pretend with me, Jacob. I don't need any grand gestures," she clipped out tersely.

His eyebrows lifted at her tone, and he frowned. "What do you mean *pretend*? It's dinner, Camille. That's all."

"You've never wanted to go to dinner before. You've never wanted to spend any time with me, why now?"

His eyes narrowed. "Look if you have plans then—"

"I don't have plans, Jacob. I just want to know *why* you suddenly want to go out with me," she said impatiently

He stared at her for several moments before he nodded, as if he was silently acknowledging that she had a point. "Because I know I have been—" he paused, and she knew he was searching for the right words to say next, "—*aloof*," he finished.

Dragging a hand through his hair he let out a deep breath. "Look, my brothers speak highly of you, and I wonder if I've misjudged you. I'd like to take you to dinner to talk, get to know you better, that's all."

She arched an eyebrow as she studied him. He seemed genuine enough, although she still didn't trust him. She nodded slowly. He was right. It *was* just dinner. It wouldn't hurt to actually talk to him.

"Alright then. Can you give me a couple of hours to finish this and then get dressed?"

"Of course. I'll just shower, change and nap while you finish up."

She stood there for several minutes, slightly perplexed after he left her apartment.

What had she just agreed to? She wanted to believe this was some kind of nefarious trap, but there was nothing about his actions or words that said it was anything more than a simple dinner.

Sitting back down at her computer she worked to finish her column. Jacob was turning out to be quite an enigma indeed.

* * * *

"You look lovely this evening."

Camille ducked her head as heat crept into her cheeks, and little jitters of pleasure glided across her skin at the compliment.

Nodding slowly, she smiled. "Thank you," she murmured softly, averting her eyes from Jacob's penetrating stare.

She lifted her menu to hide her face, trying to still the slight trembling of her hands. She scanned the menu quickly, immediately deciding on her dinner, but she continued to hold it in front of her hoping to buy herself some time.

All too quickly the waiter returned to take their orders, forcing her to relinquish her death grip on the delicate paper.

With nothing left to do *but* focus on Jacob, she slid her gaze to his face. Her heart skipped a beat as her eyes roamed over him. His stormy blue eyes held a wealth of mystery in their depths as they stared back at her. She forced herself to stifle a groan as she absorbed just how unbelievably handsome he was. Dressed in a charcoal gray suit, his raven hair brushed against the nape of his neck, while a solitary lock fell across his brow. She ached to reach her hand across the table and push the wayward strand off his gorgeous face. "Do I look lovely too?"

He'd spoken, but she'd been so wrapped up in staring at him that she'd missed his words. "I'm sorry?"

Jacob's grin grew wider. "You keep staring. I wonder if you think that I look lovely too," he teased.

She returned his grin with a warm smile. "You do," she said softly, slightly surprised by the husky lilt of her voice, before her face suddenly heated with embarrassment when she realised what she'd said. "I mean—I mean you look nice this evening." She finished. God, she was so mortified. His teasing had caught her off guard. His grins had too. He rarely smiled, and she didn't think she could handle it if he did it more often. The effect was devastating.

"Thank you," he said softly as his eyes twinkled with amusement.

She lowered her gaze, still embarrassed by her slip of tongue.

Silence hung between them as if they were both afraid to say something that would break the spell of the moment.

Unnerved by his penetrating stare, she glanced over his shoulder, but immediately regretted doing so.

"Good evenin' Ms. Camille," the man tipped his Stetson at her before pinning Jacob with a steely glare. "Downing," he bit out as if it pained him to say that one word.

She closed her eyes for just a second, struggling to calm her racing mind and wildly beating heart.

She opened her eyes then to stare into the face of Pete Rollins, the old foreman that had once worked on a ranch in Arizona before coming to hers when she was just a girl. Pete was like an uncle to her, who'd grown even more protective since the death of her father. Now with her back in Texas he'd taken it upon himself to be her self-appointed guardian. When he found out that she'd "moved in" with Jacob, he'd been furious. The entire town of Macon had been ablaze with the rumour that she and Jacob were dating. They still weren't certain how the town had decided it was Jacob and not any one of the other Downings. How they'd come up with that *particular* pairing remained a mystery, but neither one of them felt the need to say otherwise. She knew by going *out* to dinner the chances that they would spark another round of rumours was high, but she didn't care. She would rather people assume that she and Jacob were bringing an end to the Douglas and Downing feud than discover the truth — that she was the exclusive mistress to the entire Downing clan.

"Good evening, Uncle Pete. Fancy seeing you here," she said politely, hoping he wouldn't make a scene. Out of loyalty to her family, over the years he had taken up the mantle of hating the Downings and she knew that it wouldn't take much to set him off given the rumours flying about, and especially now that he'd seen her out with Jacob.

"Camille, can I have a word with you?"

She sighed inwardly knowing that he wanted to get her away from Jacob just so that he could once again rail at her for making such a disastrous mistake. She moved to tell him that they could speak later, at a more appropriate time, when Jacob stood from his seat.

She watched in horror as Jacob stepped towards old Pete, his body language commanding attention, as his eyes focused solely on the older man.

"Camille and I are trying to have a nice quiet dinner. Is this something you can discuss with her later?" Jacob's words were soft, but she could see the muscle in his jaw twitching furiously, which she knew only happened when he was angry or irritated.

"Step back, Downing. This has nothing do with you," Pete bit out, his voice rising.

She cringed inside when the restaurant suddenly grew silent.

Her frantic gaze darted between the two angry men, their postures rigid, their faces twisted with fury.

"Gentlemen, please. We're causing a scene," she hissed out just loud enough for them to hear her.

Pete hesitated for several moments before he tipped his hat. "We'll talk later then," he said, nodding his head towards her although his gaze still remained focused on Jacob.

She let out a loud sigh of relief when Pete finally stomped off and Jacob settled back into his chair.

Swinging her gaze to Jacob, she shot him a hard glare. She was mad at him for confronting Pete. "What was that about?" She demanded in a low voice, still mindful of the prying eyes and nosy ears.

Jacob shrugged. "You tell me." He said tightly, as his eyes darkened to the colour of a stormy sea. "That's *your* employee."

She stiffened at the bite in his tone. "No, that's *your* employee," she snapped back. "Last time I checked *you* still owned the Douglas ranch."

"Yes, so maybe you should tell your old foreman that since apparently he doesn't seem to realise —"

Her eyes widened in alarm. "You *cannot* fire Pete. He has been our foreman for years —"

Jacob's nostrils flared angrily. "But as you so wisely stated before it is not *your* ranch anymore." His lips curved into a sardonic grin as he leaned across the table. "Well, at least not until you've paid off your debt."

She cringed at the picture he painted with his offensive words. Despite the nature of their arrangement, she wasn't a whore and she resented his insinuation that she was. "Just like a Downing," she hissed angrily. "You greedy, manipulative, *tactless* bastard —"

Jacob's blue eyes turned to ice as his gaze grew cold. "Well I guess the apple doesn't fall far from the tree either," he said bitterly. "Considering the women in *your* family play men like pawns in a game, using your *bodies* to manipulate them."

She reared back in shock, unable to believe that he'd had the gall to bring up the bad blood between their families, and then throw *his* version of the truth in her face.

She leaned forward so that her face was only inches from his.

"You have some nerve, Jacob Downing. Your family has caused mine nothing but heartbreak and grief."

He arched one arrogant eyebrow. "I could say the same thing to you, Camille."

She shook her head. "I knew this dinner was a mistake," she said quietly, her voice barely above a whisper. Standing to her full height, she pushed back her chair.

"Camille, sit down."

She rolled her eyes at him before she spun on her heels and marched out of the restaurant, her head high.

She stood outside the restaurant on shaky legs, her body trembling with anger.

"Where the hell are you going to get a cab, you idiot?" she muttered under her breath.

This wasn't Dublin or New York or any of the other major cities she'd lived in before. No cabs were coming unless she walked back into the restaurant and called them — which she absolutely refused to do.

She knew the moment he stepped outside. The cool air carried his masculine scent directly to her and the rich heady smell of him tickled her nose.

With her back still to him, she folded her arms under her breasts, and lifted her chin a notch higher.

Without warning, she felt fingers curl around her arm from behind. A gasp of shock escaped her lips when she was suddenly dragged by her arm to the side of the restaurant, next to the parking lot. Now plunged into the dark shadows of the night, she blinked furiously as her eyes struggled to adjust to the dim lighting.

She lifted her blurry gaze to meet what she knew was the stormy eyes of the man that still held her arm. "Let go of me," she bit out as she struggled to pull her arm from his grasp, but he didn't bulge. Pushing her back against the brick wall of the building, he cornered her in. Once he had her imprisoned between the wall and his large frame, he finally released her. "I'm sorry. I was out of line back there," he whispered, his hand reaching out to caress her cheek.

She stood there, a little stunned by the gentleness she glimpsed in his eyes and the softness she felt in his touch, but she didn't let it sway her.

"What do you want from me, Jacob?"

His hand stilled against her cheek, and he tilted his head to the side to stare down at her, his expression thoughtful.

"Isn't it obvious?" he murmured huskily.

She shook her head. "No it isn't. You're always distant with me, but then you're in my bed every night—all night. Now you take me to dinner, but then you insult me. Jacob, I get it. You want revenge on my family for what my parents did to you and your family and you're using me to get it. That's fine. I agreed to the terms of the contract and I am yours physically, but I refuse to play these mind games with you."

Jacob's eyes narrowed and he held her gaze, his mouth lifting into a slight grin. "You intrigue me, Camille. At every turn you fight me, even though I still own you for the next three months."

Her nostrils flared as anger coursed through her veins. "You do not own me, Jacob Downing," she gritted out tightly.

His grin grew wider, seemingly amused by her spark of anger. "That's where you're wrong, Camille," he said softly, before he lowered his head and captured her lips with his mouth, in a slow, sensual kiss. "You belong to me in every way that a woman can belong to a man and I think you know it," he murmured softly against her lips, before claiming her mouth once again.

She moaned against his mouth, as her body responded to him, although her mind continued to struggle with his possessive words. However, his kiss soon pushed all thoughts from her mind, including the ones that had been filled with anger towards him only moments ago. Lifting her arms, she wrapped her hands around his neck, dragging him into her embrace.

His kiss grew deeper, more demanding, more urgent as he pressed his stiff erection into her stomach, rotating his hips back and forth.

Her pussy clenched at his rhythm, as it grew moist and swollen with need.

A startled cry escaped her lips, when he suddenly pressed her back deeper into the wall. Reaching under her form fitting dress, he slid his hands up her thighs. Looping his fingers under her thong, he pulled it down her legs. She smiled as she remembered he'd done that the first night they'd made love.

As soon as he had them off, he shucked them aside. Reaching for his pants, she watched numbly as he unbuttoned the fastener, and slid down his zipper.

Thought finally came back to her fuddled brain when he pulled out his large cock that was now stiff and ready. She shook her head, not quite believing he was going to make love to her against a wall, in public no less.

"Jacob," she gasped in shock when he hooked his arms behind her knees and lifted her legs. Pinned against the wall, she clung to his shoulders.

"We can't," she protested. "People will see—"

"We're in the shadows," he murmured as he brought his cock to the mouth of her moist cunt.

"Jacob, I'm serious," she moaned when he slowly began to push inside her. "People will hear."

She groaned softly when he seated himself fully inside her pussy.

"Then you'll have to be quieter than you normally are," he whispered into the crook of her neck as he began to piston his hard length in and out of her wet, warm pussy.

"Jacob," she cried out again as his hips bucked furiously against her, propelling his cock balls deep.

Through the thin material of her dress she could feel the jagged edges of the bricks as they lightly scraped against her back. She ignored the slight twinges of pain. It was a small trade-off for the pleasure that throbbed at the centre of her core. When Jacob surged inside of her on a deep thrust, she automatically tightened the muscles of her sheath around his dick, eliciting a sharp hiss from him.

"Camille," he cried out desperately as he thrust his cock into her with erratic movements. She could tell he was close to coming when his pace grew more urgent.

Tightening her arms around him she held on and threw her hips at him, meeting him thrust for thrust.

"Oh God. Oh God. Oh God," she moaned as tiny tremors surged through her pussy. "Jacob, I'm coming."

She stiffened as a wave of pleasure erupted inside of her, inflaming her skin and sending her hurling over the edge straight to utter completion. She turned her head and buried her face in Jacob's neck, muffling her hoarse screams. She trembled for several moments as her cum gushed from her pussy, drenching Jacob's cock in her wet heat.

"God, your pussy feels so good," Jacob groaned, his hips now thrusting furiously as he pumped his stiff erection into her dripping cunt. Over and over again, he stuffed his cock inside of her. She could hear his breathing coming in short bursts, as the muscles beneath her hands, bunched with tension.

His dick suddenly twitched inside of her and grew harder at the same time he let out a hoarse cry and then exploded, showering her pussy with his hot cum.

"Yes, Camille. Yes," he growled out into her neck, his hard rod still pounding wildly inside her while he emptied his load deep into her womb.

They remained locked there for several moments, their breathing laboured. Slowly, Jacob pulled back from her, letting his soft cock slide from her slippery pussy, before he lowered her feet to the ground. She patted at her dress, trying to smooth out the wrinkles, although it was no use. She glanced at Jacob who was busy tucking his wrinkled dress shirt back into his pants. A grin lifted the corners of her mouth. Anyone who saw them would know *exactly* what they had been up to just by looking at their dishevelled appearances.

"Are you ready?"

She nodded as she grasped Jacob's outstretched hand and let him guide her towards his car.

Opening the door, he helped her in before walking around to the driver's side. Once they were both settled in, she relaxed against the soft leather seat. Closing her eyes, she didn't realise that she'd fallen asleep until they arrived home and she woke up to find herself stretched out on top of her bed.

Her eyes fluttered open just in time to see Jacob tiptoeing out of her room.

"Don't go," she whispered. Her eyes still heavy with sleep.

Jacob turned to stare down at her, his gaze thoughtful. "Are you sure?"

She nodded at the same time she lifted one hand out to beckon him towards her.

In two easy strides he was back at the side of her bed.

She stared up into his face. The desire that brewed in his gaze was unmistakable. She laid there numbly watching while he quickly slipped out of his clothing. With the utmost gentleness, he settled his large body on top of hers.

Reaching up, she tangled her fingers in his soft hair and dragged him down to meet her waiting lips.

He kissed her with a hunger that belied the fact that they had just made passionate love no more than an hour ago.

With the utmost gentleness, Jacob slipped her dress from her shoulders, his lips singeing her skin with every heated kiss that he showered upon her neck, her shoulders, the upper swells of her breasts.

"Lift," he commanded softly.

She lifted up slightly so that he could work her dress down the length of her body. As soon as he got it past her feet he balled the soft fabric into his hand and carelessly tossed it aside.

She laid there for several charged moments while his eyes leisurely roamed over her body.

He frowned then.

Her heart stilled in her chest as her old insecurities came crashing back, causing her to wonder if he now frowned because he no longer found her desirable. Maybe the novelty of her overly lush figure had worn off and he was finally seeing her in a different light.

"I hate these things," he murmured as his fingers looped through the thin straps of her thong along her hips.

She glanced down her body. "My thongs?"

He nodded. "Yes. I thought you left this outside when we made love earlier."

"I couldn't leave my panties on the ground, Jacob."

"Well you should have. I thought I told you not to wear panties."

She shook her head. "You said not to when I'm here, but we were out."

"Well from now on, just don't wear *any* panties — anywhere, ever. I want you ready at all times for my cock," he whispered huskily, his eyes darkening with desire as he slipped her thong from her hips all the way down the length of her body before tossing them aside.

"Jacob, I can't leave the house without under — "

His eyebrows lifted. "Yes you can. And you will," he said firmly.

She opened her mouth to protest. He was crazy if he thought she would walk around without panties just because he wanted *easy* access at *all* times.

Before she could argue with him, he lowered his head to nibble at the soft skin against her neck.

A sharp cry escaped her lips and tingles raced down her back as her nipples hardened and her pussy began to flood with juice. She closed her eyes, giving herself over to the pleasure of his lovemaking. They could argue about her going out commando style later.

Her heartbeat quickened when Jacob slowly slipped her bra straps from her shoulders. Not bothering to unfasten the hooks, he pushed the cups down, so that her full breasts spilled forth.

"God, you're gorgeous," Jacob whispered softly, his voice sounding almost reverent.

She opened her eyes to meet his intense gaze, shocked that he wasn't staring down at her breasts. Embarrassed by his intense scrutiny, a flush of heat crept up her body. She closed her eyes again, no longer able to meet his penetrating gaze.

"Open your eyes, Camille," he demanded on a low growl.

She snapped her lids open, her stomach lurching slightly at the depth of longing that was evident in his gaze.

"I want to stare into your eyes when I enter you," he whispered softly.

She nodded slightly before she lifted her legs to wrap them around his waist.

Staring into his face, she struggled not to shut her eyes and instead focused on arching her hips off the bed as he slowly fed his cock into her dripping pussy, inch by inch.

"Jacob," she moaned and dug her nails into his taut ass, begging him with her actions to seat himself fully inside her aching pussy.

A wicked grin spread across his face before he stopped and pulled out, leaving only the head inside.

"Jacob. Please," she cried out, clutching at his ass trying to drag him back inside of her, but he held fast.

"Please what?"

"P—please make love to me," she heard herself choke out in a desperate voice she barely recognised as her own.

He smiled. "That's it?"

She shook her head in confusion. "I—I yes. I—I don't know. I don't understand."

He arched one sexy eyebrow as he stared down into her flushed face.

"So you don't want my cock?" he asked, his deep voice washing over her.

"Yes. I mean no. I mean, *yes* I *want* your cock!" God, she sounded like an idiot.

He grinned again. "Are you sure?"

She nodded.

"Yes. I'm sure," she shouted when he pulled his length all the way out of her cunt. Apparently her nod wasn't sufficient.

"Then say it."

"I just did!"

"Say it again. Say you want *my* cock."

"I want you Jacob."

Tears of frustration sprung from her eyes as he teased her by pulling back some more to place just the very tip of his dick against her opening.

"No. *Again* Camille, say you want *my* cock," he barked out, his body now vibrating as he barely held on to his control.

"I want your cock, Jacob."

"How bad?" he asked softy as he inched his way deeper inside her.

"Jacob, you're killing me—" she whined.

"Say it, Camille," he said tightly.

"I want you more than I've wanted any other man. I want your cock more than I've wanted anything in this entire *world*," she screamed out the last word when Jacob plunged deep inside of her on one smooth, hard stroke.

"Jesus, Camille. You are so wet. So tight," he groaned out as he fucked her with hard strokes.

Slamming into her cunt over and over again with deep pounding thrusts, Jacob rode her hard as his balls slapped against her pussy.

Clinging to him, she tightened her legs around his hips and her arms around his neck. The thrust of his hips was so forceful that he lifted her off of the bed every time he entered her, sending the headboard crashing against the wall on every thrust.

"Camille," he rasped out. He kept calling her name as he fucked her with desperate, hungry thrusts.

There was a wildness about his lovemaking that had never been there before. As if he was trying to brand her with each stroke inside her.

She shook her head back and forth as inarticulate screams spilled from her lips. Unable to meet his gaze any longer she let her head drift back against the pillow, moments before her climax exploded through her body.

"*Jacob*," she screamed into the night as her toes curled and her thighs began to shake as sticky cum coated his cock until it poured like rivers from her pussy to stain the bed.

"Yes, Camille. Shit," Jacob shouted out moments before his cock erupted inside of her and streams of milky semen shot to the back of her cunt, deep into her womb. Several loads of ejaculate spurted from him until her channel filled up and some seeped out of her hole to join her waiting juices on the bed.

"That's it, Camille. Milk my cock with your tight pussy," Jacob murmured against her ear while he continued to work his cock inside her with leisurely strokes. His hips pumped slowly back and forth until he was finally spent and collapsed atop her with a single shudder.

Unlocking her legs from around his waist, she planted her feet against the bed and held Jacob in her arms, stroking his sweat drenched back.

"Damn, Camille. That was amazing," he murmured, before he rolled off of her only to drag her into the crook of his body.

"Mmmmm. That was." She smiled sleepily, turning her face into the hollow of his neck.

He chuckled before he placed a soft kiss against her forehead. "Go to sleep, beautiful," he whispered tenderly.

A soft sigh escaped her lips before she quickly drifted off to sleep.

Chapter Four

Camille's eyelids slowly fluttered open as she awoke to a flurry of tender caresses and heated kisses.

"Good morning, sleepy head."

She curled her lips into a small smile as she stared into Jason's handsome face.

"Good morning to you too," she said sleepily before she shifted her gaze around the room.

"He's gone."

Startled, she gasped softly, her head whipping around to meet the eyes of Jeff, surprised that he'd read her thoughts, as a rueful smile lifted the corners of her mouth.. When she'd awoken earlier to grab a quick shower, he'd joined her and afterwards they'd both crawled back into bed to sleep, but at some point he'd managed to slip out without her knowing.

Jeff returned her smile with a knowing gaze.

"Jacob doesn't share very well—"

"And that includes you," Jason interrupted.

"*Especially* you," Jeff finished.

She nodded, still too sleepy to understand *exactly* what their words meant.

She didn't have the chance to dwell on their words for much longer when Jason's mouth fastened around one of her nipples, sending all of her thoughts scattering like leaves in the wind.

A soft moan was dragged from her lips when he lifted his hand to massage her other breast.

Her pussy began to throb when he rotated his tongue around the stiffened peak, before he latched his mouth around it again to suck her flesh. Goosebumps popped out across her skin as her body began to go up in flames.

She let out a moan of protest when he lifted his head from her breasts.

A mischievous grin spread across his face before he took his large hands and cupped her breasts, lifting them high and pushing them together so that he could devour them.

He shot out his tongue to flick across both nipples, before he dipped his head to suckle one nipple and then the other. Her eyes slid closed and her head fell back against the pillow as the pleasurable sensations wound their way through her body.

Through her fog of arousal she could hear Jason making loud suctioning noises each time he released one nipple for the other. He continued to worship her breasts with his mouth, before he eagerly slid down her body, raining a trail of kisses against her stomach, down one leg and up the other, before placing several against the soles of her feet. By the time he made it to her bare mound, her body was humming with need.

With gentle movements he spread her thighs to give himself a better view of her glistening cunt. He sucked in a sharp breath, probably shocked by just how wet she was.

"Jason," she hissed when he stroked his tongue slowly through the folds of her pussy, licking up her cream.

She reached around to tangle her hands in his hair as he ravaged her pussy with his teasing strokes.

"Jason, please," she begged.

Vibrations drummed against her sensitive flesh as he chuckled softly against her mound, moments before he roughly shoved his tongue inside of her.

"Ahh," she cried out, her back shooting off the bed.

Holding her legs wide open, Jason plunged his tongue inside her hole with deep, probing strokes.

His searching tongue caused her cunt to gush more juice as her arousal grew. Yet she knew that unless he stroked her bud, she would never come.

Lifting one hand from his head, she reached around to finger her clit, the sensations eliciting a moan from her lips.

She cried out sharply when suddenly Jason gripped her wrist and cast her hand aside. Shifting up slightly, he slipped his tongue from her cunt, only to replace it with two fingers, before his lips latched on to her clit, sucking hard.

Flares of heat shot from her pussy and spread throughout her entire body. Her thighs began to tremble as her pussy pulsed and vibrated.

"Jason," she screamed out hoarsely when he nipped her clit with his teeth, sending her hurtling over the edge. Her belly tightened and she thrashed about wildly against the bed, as her climax roared through her sending her juices pouring from her slit.

Still in the throes of her climax, Jason flipped her over onto her stomach, lifted her up to her hands and knees, and drove into her from behind.

"Camille," he groaned as his hips began to move, propelling his cock deep into her still spasming pussy over and over again.

Her eyes snapped open when she felt a gentle hand cup her chin. She had completely forgotten about Jeff.

He laid down on the bed and slid beneath her so that her palms rested on the outside of his thighs, his bobbing erection lining up just below her head. She shifted down onto her elbows and took him inside her mouth.

A series of sharp hisses and moans erupted from all of them at the same time. With her ass high in the air, the new position allowed Jason, to drill her deeper. The sensations of having him fill her so deeply caused waves of pleasure to slide across her skin. At the same time, her breasts, brushed against Jeff's hairy thighs, causing her nipples to tingle from the rough feel of his coarse hair. Apparently, Jeff also liked the feel of her soft breasts caressing his thighs because his moans grew louder.

She released him from her mouth to encircle his shaft with a single hand and pump gently. A bead of precum gathered between the slit in the head of his cock and she flicked her tongue across it, lapping it up.

Jeff's eyes clenched shut as he tangled his hand deeper into her wild hair, his fingertips pressing into her scalp.

She slowly took him into her mouth once again, until his large dick pressed against the back of her throat.

His fingers gripped her hair tighter as she bobbed her head up and down, sucking his cock deeply. His hips instinctively lurched off the bed, feeding her his hard length in shallow strokes. She pressed one hand against his hips to steady herself and slipped her other hand between his legs to massage the heavy sacs that lay nestled at the base of his cock.

"Oh shit," Jeff grunted out as she quickened her pace, her mouth suctioning him harder while her hand rotated his balls in the palm of her hand with deft movements.

From behind, Jason's thrusts grew harder, pushing her deeper onto Jeff's cock and she struggled not to gag. She could tell Jason was close by his wild and furious pounding as his balls slammed hard against her pussy. Leaning over her, his chest brushed against her back, as he pummelled her pussy with vigorous strokes.

She pushed back her hips, meeting his wild thrusts.

Plunging deeply within her, he buried his length inside her sheath one last time before he stiffened.

"*Camille*," he roared out then he shuddered uncontrollably, moments before his cock twitched inside her and warm semen pooled inside her cunt as he flooded the condom that separated them.

He continued to spurt his cum inside her and she wondered in the back of her mind if the thin latex would hold, but that thought was immediately cast aside, when Jeff dug his hand deeper into her tender scalp, using her head to guide her mouth up and down his cock.

She struggled to keep pace with him, as his hips jerked off the bed, his movements frenzied.

A loud roar rumbled from Jeff at the same time hot, wet liquid poured into her mouth. He tightened his hold on her head, holding her still while his hips bucked furiously beneath her as he emptied himself down her throat. She worked her lips and throat, struggling to swallow each jet of his semen.

She milked his cock with her mouth for several long moments, until he finally stopped shooting his load between her lips.

After she swallowed every last drop, she lifted her mouth from his softening erection to roll over and collapse onto the bed.

She had barely been awake when they arrived, and she could feel herself growing weary again.

She distinctly remembered them kissing her against the lips, but the rest was a blur.

When she awoke again, hours later, she was alone in her room.

* * * *

Jacob clasped Camille's small hand in his and held it firmly. She tensed at first before she slowly relaxed against him. He knew he'd caught her off guard with the intimate gesture, but under the spell of the setting sun, he'd ached to touch her. He wanted much more than to just hold her hand, but for now he would have to be content with having her fingers curl around his palm.

They strolled hand and hand across the green fields of his family ranch just watching the waning day give way to night.

"Do you think our parents would be happy that we were *closer*?"

Jacob stopped to stare down at her. She worried her bottom lip between her teeth and he could tell she was nervous.

"You mean that we've worked to bring an end to the feud?"

She nodded. Her eyes were so trusting as she held his gaze, but he couldn't lie to her.

"My father would be pleased that I've made this effort, but I can't stand here and tell you that I still don't think about the past."

The light in her eyes vanished and she tried to tug her hand from his, but he gripped her tighter. He could tell she was disappointed by his words.

"Jacob, I'm sorry for what my family did to you, but don't you think it's time to move on?" she asked quietly, her gaze sliding to the ground.

His nostrils flared in anger, but he held his temper in check. If they got into an argument now, he knew she would never open up to him again, and he desperately felt they needed to talk about this.

"I'm sorry Camille, but that's easier said than done. You don't know how hard it was for me to try and keep my family together, my family business intact and still try to learn all that I could as I grieved the death of my father. Your parents, but especially your father, played a key role in making my life a living hell in the years after dad died. I can't forgive him for that."

She swallowed deeply as she lifted her gaze to his face. "I can understand that." Several seconds ticked before she blew out a long breath and said softly, "I know what you think, but my mother loved your father. She never betrayed him."

Jacob gritted his teeth together trying to keep an angry retort from flying out. Even if he believed that Adel hadn't betrayed his father, which for the sake of Camille he was more open to accepting that notion than he'd ever been before, that still didn't absolve her father of his crimes.

She lifted her eyes to meet his gaze, her eyes shimmering with compassion. He stilled when she slid her hand up to stroke his cheek.

"You can punish me for the sins of my family, better yet, the sins of my father, but even after this is all over you'll still never be happy."

The look of sadness in her eyes gave him pause and he cupped her hand against his face not knowing what else to say or do.

"Jacob, it doesn't have to be this way between us. If you could just let go of the past...."

"What?" He asked when her voice trailed off.

She shook her head. "I—I don't know." She sighed. "I just know that my mother would have been happy to see us togeth—call an end to this feud."

He narrowed his gaze and studied her face. Her eyes were glued to the ground—*again,* and he knew that she was embarrassed by her slip. She'd almost said that they were *together.*

Were they? He knew there was something going on between them, but with his brothers in the picture, it was difficult to say with certainty that what she felt for him was any different from what she felt towards the rest of his brothers. There was also the issue of his inability to let go of the past, as she so rightly pointed out.

He'd never even considered trying to work through his bitterness. He'd never had a reason to, but now he had a reason standing right before him. He wondered what could happen between them if he actually worked on his issues and his brothers weren't in the way. Could they discover a deeper level to their relationship? The thought caused a curious warmth to settle in the pit of his stomach, and he stiffened when he realised what had just happened. He was starting to fall for her. It was unbelievable, but it was true. The thought scared him to death and he felt like he'd just been doused in a bucket of ice water.

"We better get back," he blurted out abruptly. He hadn't been prepared for the possibility that he could fall for her. Now he needed some time to consider what was happening between them, and he needed to do that *alone.*

He practically dragged her back to her apartment. He couldn't get away from her fast enough. As soon as he deposited her inside her place, he turned to leave, but he stopped when she placed a gentle hand against his shoulder.

"Jacob, don't leave," she said softly.

He closed his eyes as he struggled to tamp down his growing arousal at the husky lilt of her sensual voice.

"I—I should really go. I have a couple of business plans that I should look over—"

"Stay with me tonight. Please."

His heart squeezed in his chest and in that moment he knew he could not deny her plea.

With a frustrated groan at his powerlessness when it came to her, he whirled around and dragged her into his arms to crush his lips against hers in a bruising kiss. Slipping his tongue inside the moist cavern of her mouth he devoured her while his hands roamed all over her body.

Heat pooled at the centre of his groin as he felt his length grow rigid within the confines of his jeans. He tore his lips from hers long enough to rip off her summer tank top and roughly tug her jeans past her full lips and down her shapely legs.

He settled on his haunches to help her step out of her pants but lingered down there to place a smattering of kisses against her ankles. When she clutched at his hair he slowly slid up her body, placing a trail of hot wet kisses against the soft skin of her legs and inner thighs. When he reached her bare pussy he dragged in the scent of her through his nose. Burying his face in her mound he shot out his wet tongue to slide it through the moist folds of her cunt.

A sharp gasp tore from her lips as her legs buckled. He held her hips firmly to keep her from falling as he stood to his full height.

They'd spent many nights together making love, their strokes and caresses slow and unhurried, but this was not be one of those nights. There was an urgency in the air that called to them, demanding that their bodies satisfy the primitive urge to physically connect with another human being.

Jacob hurriedly backed them towards her breakfast bar, pushing her flush against the low counter.

"Turn around and bend over," he rasped out.

She nodded slowly before she obeyed his command and turned around to bed over the bar, her hands flat against its top.

With one hand, he massaged the full globes of her naked ass, while the other quickly undid the fastening and zipper of his jeans. He stopped stroking her ass long enough to hastily push his pants down to mid thigh, and then wrap his hand around his fully erect cock.

His breathing was ragged as his held his dick in his hand, struggling not to come before he could even get inside her. He took his cock and poked at her tiny hole, testing her readiness. When wet warmth seeped from her slit to coat the tip of his dick he knew she was more than ready. Closing his eyes, he sank his cock inside her on a single thrust.

She cried out his name, her back arching like a bow at the same time he released a feral growl.

He pushed past the clenching muscles of her cunt until his balls met her flesh and he was seated fully inside her moist sheath. Her sticky warmth surrounded him as her cunt gripped him like a tight fist. He reached out to seize her hips as he rocked his hips forward to tunnel his cock inside her with fast, hard strokes.

The heavy sacs of his balls slapped against her skin on each stroke as her pussy grew slick with juice causing his thrusts to grow wild and frantic as he struggled not to slide out of her slippery pussy.

"That's it, Jacob. Fuck me," she moaned as he pounded into her from behind.

His thrusts grew more frenzied as he slammed his cock into her with urgent strokes. He released her hips to grip her shoulder with one hand while the other slid around her waist to dip between her legs and rotate her clit between his fingers.

"Jacob," she screamed, as she jerked against him, pushing her ass back with each thrust so that he buried himself deeper inside her with every stroke.

He could feel his balls tightening, signalling that he was close. He fingered her clit harder and faster, in rhythm with his pounding cock. She quickened her own pace, meeting each hard thrust every time she shoved her ass against him.

A loud cry echoed off the walls at the same time her cunt clamped down around him. Her hips bucked furiously as she impaled herself on his dick with wild strokes. The wet warmth of her climax surrounded his cock, trickling from her hole to coat the nest of hair that covered his balls. With her pulsating hot, wet cunt milking his cock, he finally gave in to his own shattering release.

Digging his nails into her shoulder, he held her still as he rammed his cock into her with four hard strokes before he clenched his eyes shut. As his sticky ejaculate shot out from his dick to bathe the inner walls of her cunt, he threw his head back and released a hoarse shout of completion.

For several long moments, his body twitched and jerked as the aftershocks of his climax continued to wrack him. When he was finally able to draw in a normal breath he slid out of her and pulled his pants up.

On shaky legs, they both wobbled to the bedroom where they collapsed onto the bed. In seconds, Camille was fast asleep, in his arms. He held her against him as he laid awake, staring at her ceiling.

Making love to her when he was already emotionally raw had been a mistake. In a span of hours she'd chipped away at some of the ice that had surrounded his heart since the day his father died. He wasn't sure if he was ready to deal with all of the emotions she'd awakened inside him so he needed to put some distance between them to gather his thoughts. He needed to figure out where this was headed and what he truly wanted from her. He had a lot of things to consider and he knew if he didn't get some space he would end up doing what he'd done tonight—fall into her arms and into her bed. They were perfectly compatible inside the bedroom, but what about outside of it? He couldn't answer that question, which is why he needed to take a break from Camille.

Chapter Five

If she hadn't forgotten her scarf she would have missed the note entirely. Lifting the folded piece of paper into her hands, she noticed Jacob's handwriting immediately. Quickly she scanned the note, only to frown when she finished. A disappointed sigh escaped her lips as she threw the note away and left her apartment.

Bounding down the steps, she hurried towards the stables. Turning the corner, she smiled when she saw Jackson standing there dressed in his chaps all set to ride.

He returned her smile, his eyes apologetic.

"Jacob *really* wanted to ride with you, but an equipment purchase came through in Dallas and he had to head there immediately. He's really sorry."

She nodded, unable to hide the disappointment on her face. "I know. He left a note."

"If you don't want to go—"

She shook her head. "No, I have been looking forward to this all week."

Jackson hesitated. "But I'm not Jacob," he said simply.

She wanted to pretend that she didn't know what he meant, but she did. She'd been their mistress for four months, and somehow in that time, they'd all managed to move beyond their mutual distrust and establish a deeper connection. Since she'd gone to dinner with Jacob just a month ago, things had changed the most between them — and all for the better. She thought after last night they'd broken through another barrier in their relationship, but now he was gone and she couldn't talk to him to find out if she'd just imagined it all.

She shook her head trying to push aside the thoughts as she cursed herself silently. *I keep doing that.* She kept inventing a relationship between her and Jacob that really didn't exist. Even last night, she'd slipped up and almost blurted out that they were *together*, but that was so far from the truth. This *thing* between them was not permanent, more importantly it wasn't even a *real* affair. *He shares me with his brothers for godssakes!* She also wasn't completely convinced that he still didn't have a hidden agenda in all of this. She was still having a hard time trusting him completely, but at the same time, she couldn't seem to stop the racing of her heart every time she saw him.

Firmly pushing all thoughts of Jacob from her head, she turned to Jackson. There would be plenty of time to worry about what the hell she was doing with Jacob later. Right now, all she wanted to do was ride. A warm smile spread across her face.

"Let's go Jackson," she said, ignoring his comment as she lifted herself onto Cobalt, the pretty black mare.

Jackson nodded, as a grin spread across his face and he lifted himself onto his own mount. As soon as he was seated she took off, racing across the wide expanse of arid earth that stretched for miles and miles.

She inhaled deeply as the fresh air whipped about her face, her hair fanning out behind her as she rode with reckless abandon. She hadn't been on a horse since she was in college. It was an amazing, exhilarating experience. She didn't realise how much she missed riding until Jacob's invitation. As she flew across the Downing ranch, she promised herself that she would make a point to ride more often. The feeling of freedom was indescribable as she gave herself over to the sensation of flying. Laughter bubbled up inside her, finally breaking free. It had been a long time since she felt so happy, so carefree — and again she had Jacob to thank for bringing back some of the light in her eyes. She hadn't realised how much she truly needed to be back on a horse, but apparently Jacob had. His ability to read her and her moods was scary at times. He just had a way of anticipating her needs and her wants, sometimes before even she could.

After what felt like hours, she dug her heels into Cobalt's flanks, urging her to slow down. Whipping her head around, she signalled to Jackson and he nodded back. She trotted towards a small stream and dismounted before tethering Cobalt to a nearby tree so that she could take a break.

Slipping down onto the grass, she leaned back against a large tree, enjoying the comfort of the shade as the scorching Texas sun beat down upon them. Drawing her legs up, she wrapped her arms around them, holding herself in a tight ball.

"You look so much like your mother. It's amazing."

The blood froze in her veins and she immediately stiffened at the latent meaning in his words. As a child, he'd probably seen her mother in his home on more than one occasion and knew her face well.

"I'm sorry. I—I didn't mean. I mean...that was stupid of me to say."

She turned to stare at Jackson. His face was flushed red with embarrassment.

She offered him a reassuring smile. "It's okay. It's no secret," she whispered, before turning once again to stare out at the rolling hills of dry grass.

"Dad did his best to be discreet about their relationship, and I was young then so I really don't know much. I just remember how everything changed after she was gone," he said as he sat down next to her.

She glanced at him. "Do you believe the rumours—that your dad died of a broken heart?"

Jackson nodded, his eyes now distant as he followed her gaze towards the golden horizon. "He did. He was so lost after she died." He let out a deep sigh. "I never really listened to what other people said— that she used dad, although for awhile I too wasn't absolutely certain that she didn't do what everyone said she did. But I know dad certainly didn't listen to the words of gossipers. He loved her."

She fixed her gaze upon Jackson. "Jacob doesn't believe that. That my mother didn't set him up."

Jackson turned to stare at her, his eye gaze thoughtful.

"Jacob still blames your mom for dad's death. He thinks her supposed betrayal killed him. The rest of us always had our doubts, but Jacob was closest to dad so it hit him the hardest. The rest of us were always willing to believe that your mother wasn't guilty."

"My mother didn't give Titan Corporations insider information. She was framed after her death, Jackson, I know it. I'm almost certain my father did it so that in death he could finally do what he hadn't been able to do during her life. Destroy her love for your father," she said quietly and ducked her head.

"You don't have to try to convince me." He let out a ragged breath. "It wasn't until you came here that I finally realised it was time to let go of the past. What our parents did or didn't do has nothing to do with us." He shrugged. "Jacob seems to be the only person who thinks differently."

A bitter smile lifted her lips. "I know. We've argued about that a few times. He seems to think the women in my family are all whores and users," she said dryly.

Jackson sighed. "He can be a bit self righteous at times."

She smiled at the truth of Jackson's words, but didn't respond to his comment.

"My mother loved your father. I know she would never have done anything to hurt him."

"I know. And you being here has helped the rest of us realise this. Maybe Jacob will too — one day."

She furrowed her brow as she stared back at him. "I don't get it. If he hates my family so much then why am I here? Why not just refuse to sell back my land and move on? Why bring me into his home, and pretend that he feels anything but disdain towards me?"

A small smile lifted the corners of his mouth. "I don't know how or *why* Jacob came up with this particular arrangement. At the time, we all had our reservations about his idea." His eyes flashed with mischief as a wicked grin crossed his face. "But then you walked through that door and the rest of us were just so smitten with you that none of us protested."

She snorted at his words, trying to keep her eyes from rolling. She didn't believe him for one second.

"I know your bastard of an ex-husband tried to convince you otherwise, but you're beautiful, and believe me we didn't agree to Jacob's plan until *after* you walked into our office that day," he added when she lifted a single brow, her expression sceptical.

She shook her head at his words, still not quite believing that he was telling the truth — that they *all* desired her in some way.

"It's true. We thought Jacob was crazy for even suggesting it, but then you strolled in and all of a sudden we were convinced that it was a brilliant idea." He chuckled softly. "I know you may not believe it, but I can assure you, what Jacob feels for you is *far* from hate. I think he's falling for you, but he can't quite convince himself to let go of the past long enough to admit it."

She shook her head. "Jacob isn't *falling* for me. I doubt I've had any positive influence on him — at least when it comes to his views regarding my family."

His eyes twinkled with amusement. "You would be surprised by just how much power you hold over my brother."

As they rode back towards the house, Jackson's words haunted her. She was less convinced than he was. Jacob may not still *hate* her *or* her family, but she knew damn well he wasn't falling for her either. With Jackson's words ringing in her head, she was now more confused than ever.

* * * *

Her concerns about her relationship with Jacob continued to haunt her two weeks later. She hadn't seen him since he'd left for Dallas. And she was now pretty certain that he was purposely staying out of town in order to avoid having to see her, and that just really pissed her off.

She didn't know what his deal was, but she hated that he'd shut her out when it seemed as if they were just making progress. He'd called several times while he was away. While she was cordial when they spoke, in no way did she overflow with the enthusiasm she actually felt whenever she heard his voice. In truth, she was hurt and angry with him, and just wasn't in the mood for pleasantries when so much lay unspoken just beneath the surface.

She could hear the confusion in his voice at her distant tone when they spoke, but he held back from questioning her. She was glad that he did. She wasn't sure how she would answer him. She didn't know what was happening between them and it scared her. She wanted to let down her guard with him, but she just didn't trust him — and the more time she spent away from him the more convinced she became that she shouldn't.

She shook her head trying to clear her mind and lifted her glass of wine to her lips. She would not ruin her celebration dinner with thoughts of Jacob. She'd come to Houston two days ago to enter contract negotiations with a publisher. Impressed with her column, they'd offered her a contract to write a self-help book for divorced women, looking to enjoy life and their new found *singledom*. At times she felt like such a fraud as a columnist because she hadn't begun to live that life until recently, and yet she wrote about it each and every week. Still, fraud or not, she'd secured a book deal, so she'd decided to treat herself to dinner and lots of booze that night.

She lowered her head to scan the menu when suddenly a chill slithered down her spine. She instantly looked up. Her eyes widened and she clutched the menu tighter as her gaze zeroed in on a familiar face. She quickly lowered her head, shielding her face with the menu.

"That bastard," she muttered to herself as she peaked from behind the menu, her eyes following his every movement as he escorted his stunning blonde date to their table in a secluded section on the other side of the restaurant.

Her hands began to tremble while her heart beat frantically inside her chest.

She remembered in their last conversation that he'd said he would be travelling to Houston for a few days before returning home.

She frowned. He'd left out the part where he would be visiting his girlfriend in the process.

She stared transfixed at the stunning couple, her blood boiling with anger when he leaned towards the woman, his eyes riveted on her as he laughed at something she said. A pang of jealousy ripped through her as she watched them. Jacob sat across from the lovely woman, seemingly completely relaxed and comfortable, wearing an easy smile. It was obvious the two were *intimately* familiar with each other to have such a rapport.

"The bastard," she hissed again as she threw down her menu and stood up. Opening her purse she placed a bill on the table to cover her glass of wine, before she turned on her heel and stormed out of the restaurant. As she rode in the back of the cab to her hotel, tears burned the backs of her eyes, but she refused to cry.

She was not Jacob's woman, so there was no reason to feel betrayed. She was his mistress, there to serve his sexual needs. That was her place in his life, so she could not question him if he had other women in his life. Still the pain sliced through her like a sharp knife.

She'd known all along that Jacob had set out to hurt her. She just never realised that it would come in such a classic form.

****

Camille's breasts jiggled wildly as she bounced on Jackson's cock. Throwing her head back, a long moan escaped her lips.

"Camille," he growled as he clutched her ass in his firm hands.

She opened her eyes to stare down into his face. His eyes were shut and his jaw was clenched tight as the muscles in his neck and shoulders bunched and strained while he valiantly tried to stave off his orgasm.

"Let go Jackson. Come inside me." She cried out, as she bounced her ass against him, riding his cock harder, taking him deeper inside her.

Her words sent him over the edge as a loud roar rumbled through his chest, before he erupted in a hoarse shout of completion. Pumping his cock up into her on short, stabbing strokes, his seed poured into the condom that encased his hard length buried deep inside her.

She followed right behind him, screaming his name as she came on a tortured moan.

Exhausted, she slumped forward, her head resting against his chest.

"I thought you weren't feeling well."

A startled yelp tore past her lips. Whipping her head towards the door, her shocked gaze collided with Jacob's angry one.

She swallowed deeply, before her eyes narrowed to angry slits.

"I wasn't," she snapped as she shifted off of Jackson. She watched his eyes follow her nude form. The desire that burned in his gaze caused her to shiver, but she ignored the soft tingles of pleasure as she reached for her silk robe and shrugged it on.

Folding her arms under her breasts, she stood before Jacob.

"What do you want?" She asked, almost wincing at the icy tone of her voice.

Jacob didn't miss the chilly edge in her voice either because his eyebrows instantly snapped upwards.

"I came to see how you were doing. But I can see that you're feeling just fine," he muttered dryly, his cold eyes sliding over her with derision.

She stiffened.

Abruptly he spun on his heels and stalked off. She followed him out. Her heart skipped a beat when she saw him dump a large brown paper bag on her kitchen table before slamming out of her apartment door.

She crept to the table and peaked inside the bag. Waves of guilt washed over her when she saw that he'd brought an array of soups and DVDs to help her feel better.

She hadn't felt sick before, but she did now. She was not a cruel person, but for the past two weeks that's exactly what she'd been to Jacob, and it was wearing on her. She cared for him, and the more he extended himself, despite her rejection, the worse she felt. Yet every time she felt herself softening towards him, the mental picture of him escorting the gorgeous blonde to dinner flashed into her head.

"I don't know what he did to you, but if I know my brother, he isn't going to take your rejection much longer."

She spun around to see Jackson standing in her living room, now fully dressed.

She let out a long sigh and turned her back to him. She didn't feel like discussing this with him.

"I have to go, but remember what I said. Jacob has too much pride to allow you to just cast him aside."

She grimaced at his choice of words. "I'm not casting him aside."

He kissed her deeply for several moments before he leaned back and said. "Well that's not how it looks to the rest of us. Trust me, if I thought Jacob would let you go, I would be the first one to cheer, but I know that it isn't in his nature to let something he wants slip from his grasp so easily," he said, quietly before he turned from her and strolled out of her apartment, leaving her even more confused than she normally was as she stared at the closed door.

Jacob didn't want her, at least not in the way Jackson hinted at. What did he mean *by he'd be the first to cheer if Jacob let her go*? The way Jackson talked, one would think that they *both* cared about her. Jackson was a wonderful man, and while she did care for him, she knew her feelings for him would never rival what she felt for Jacob. But Jacob was a lost cause. He belonged to someone else, but he was too much of a bastard to just come out and say it. No, he continued to play these games, pretending that he cared as he strung her along, but she was done with him and his games. Contract or not, she refused to allow him to use her. Now all she had to do was figure out a way to make it through the last month of her contract without him touching her.

Chapter Six

Jacob flung open the door to enter his bedroom before slamming it shut with a thunderous crash. He wanted to rush back into Camille's apartment and shake her he was so furious with her. More importantly he was furious with himself.

He'd let his guard down and let her in, and now he felt like a fool. She'd been distant ever since he'd gone away on business. He knew despite the time they'd spent together that she was still having a hard time trusting him. He couldn't blame her. He was struggling with his own trust issues towards her as well. He'd thought they'd been making progress though, but when he returned from Houston she'd not only been distant, she'd been cold.

He'd made a mistake by leaving so abruptly without an explanation, but he'd thought it was for the best at the time. They both needed time away from each other to reflect on what was happening between them. He'd spent the time apart doing just that and had returned from his trip realising he wanted to pursue a *real* relationship with

Camille. He was ready to face the demons of their murky past and work to let it all go if that meant he and Camille could build a relationship together. She on the other hand had come to an entirely different realisation during their time apart.

He'd only been gone for a few weeks but in that short time she'd apparently replaced him with Jackson, since her affection now centred solely on him.

He clutched his hands into tight fists as jealousy gripped him. He never should have left her alone with Jackson. His brother was falling in love with her too, and now it would seem the feeling was mutual.

He flopped down onto his bed and dropped his head in his hands. Everything about this contract had gone all wrong, and now he wanted out. He had grown to care for her, more than he wanted to, and certainly more than he should. He had no doubt that at the end of the month she would take the deed to her property in her hands and walk away from him and his ranch without looking back. He would be powerless to stop her. He dreaded the thought that when she left she would carry Jackson in her heart and not him.

How had he allowed this to happen? How had she crawled inside his heart without him knowing it? Was this how his father had felt about Adel? Did he crave her to the point that he was willing to accept that she would never leave her husband to be with him? Did she have such a powerful influence over his dad that he hadn't even cared?

He'd never understood why if his father loved Adel as he'd claimed, that he'd never insisted she leave Earl. But now he was starting to get the picture. The Douglas women obviously had the power to cast a spell over men to the point that they would say or do anything just to keep them, in any way they could, because he was certainly about to do everything in his power to keep Camille.

Whether Camille realised it or not, she belonged to him. Her body certainly knew that, now all he had to do was sway her heart and mind because he had no intention of losing her, not to Jackson, not to any man.

* * * *

Camille's hands balled into fists as she stood there trembling with rage.

"You're just like your father. You take what's not yours, heedless of the consequences, lashing out when you don't get what you *really* want."

Jacob's blue eyes hardened. "For someone who wants *me* to let go of the past, you're apparently having a hard time doing it yourself," he bit out, his voice dripping with ice. "Besides, this has nothing to do with my father. You're just trying to change the subject because you can't face that you're not a woman of your word."

With no defence against the truth of his words she lashed out at him. "I hate you," she spat.

"We had a deal Camille, and you're not holding up your end," he said smoothly, clearly unfazed by her bitter words.

She shook her head. "Yes I am."

His jaw tightened. "You only sleep with my brothers."

"That *is* what I was commanded to do," she said icily.

"And me as well," his voice was low as he bit out the words through clenched teeth.

She shrugged then. "I can't help it if every time you stop by, I'm tired. You need to plan better."

His eyes narrowed. "See, I don't believe you're tired at all, which is why I'm enforcing the contract."

"No. You're *forcing* me to sleep with you or else you're going to renege on our agreement."

His eyes turned cold as he stared down at her. "You agreed to the terms. If you can't fulfil your end then the contract is null and void."

She shook her head again, her blood boiling with rage.

"You are a spoiled, selfish bastard who never learned how to deal with rejection."

"I'm just restating the terms."

"Fuck you and your terms," she shouted before she turned and stormed out of his office.

Furious, she stomped out of the house and hopped into her car.

She drove the ten minutes it took to get to the Douglas ranch. Piling out of her car, she strolled towards the low wooden fence and just stood there staring out at the endless stretches of land that was her family legacy. Tears slipped down her cheeks as she seriously considered walking away from Jacob and his demands.

She couldn't do it. She couldn't lose what rightfully belonged to her family because of her stupid pride. He was right. She'd agreed to his ridiculous terms. She only had one month left. She could see this through to the very end.

* * * *

"Where have you been?"

She jumped at the unexpected voice. She'd come in through the front door of the house instead of through her apartment garage because it was more well lit and she hated the dark garage at night. Even with the small light, she found it creepy. She now regretted her decision. Closing the door, she met Jacob's questioning gaze.

"What? Did you add another clause to the contract that I have to check in now? You must have done that while I was gone," she said, her voice dripping with sarcasm.

She watched as he exhaled a deep breath, before dragging his hand through his dark hair.

"I was worried about you. We didn't part on a good note. I just thought..." His voice trailed off.

She studied his face. He really did look worried. After she left her ranch, she went into town to do some window shopping and decided to eat dinner there. She'd been gone for several hours, but she didn't even stop to think for a moment that anyone would miss her, let alone worry.

Although she was still angry with him, her eyes softened a bit. "You thought I'd left for good," she finished for him. She shook her head. "No, I'm not leaving," she whispered softly.

God, she missed him so much. Her heart leapt in her chest as he stared down at her. She ached to run her hands across his jaw where she could see the hint of a shadow, knowing it would softly scrape her sensitive skin.

"I'll walk you to your room," he said finally.

She nodded as she followed behind him, trying to hide the smile that spread across her face. They were inside the house. What did he possibly think could happen to her on her way to her apartment?

Once outside her apartment, he twisted the key in the door and stepped aside to usher her in.

"Goodnight."

She turned to face him, surprised that he didn't follow her inside.

"Goodnight," she replied. She stared at the door after he shut it behind him. She stood there for several moments irritated with herself for the disappointment that his unexpected departure caused inside her. She should have been relieved, but she wasn't.

* * * *

"Jackson," Camille screamed out as her orgasm surged through her. Her pussy gripped Jackson's cock as cum flowed from her hole, coating his dick, to pool beneath her.

Jackson groaned loudly, his thrusts growing harder.

She wound her legs around Jackson's waist as he slammed his cock deeper inside her.

Over and over, he buried his hard length inside her, balls deep. Clutching at her hips, he pounded her pussy with hard, fast strokes.

"Jackson," she called out in warning moments before she felt him stiffen above her.

He let out a low curse before he abruptly pulled out of her. Gripping his cock in his hand, he pumped his shaft with three hard strokes before he sprayed his hot cum all over her stomach.

He kneeled before her, his eyes shut tight, while the strained muscles in his neck rippled and flexed beneath his skin as he struggled to calm his ragged breathing.

Finally, he opened his eyes.

"I'm sorry Camille. I didn't mean to lose control like that."

"I know, Jackson," she said softly as she kissed him gently on the cheek before lifting herself off the bed. She nodded towards her bathroom. "I need to clean up real quick. If you want, you can use the other bathroom in the hall," she said before slipping inside.

She'd barely finished drying off from washing up when she heard low angry voices coming from the hallway. *Jacob?*

With quiet steps, she ducked out of the bathroom and quickly donned a robe. Creeping to the door, she leaned against it shielding herself from view.

Craning her neck, she listened intently.

"What the hell was that?" Jacob demanded angrily

"I know. I just lost control."

"That's unacceptable Jackson."

"Look I'm sorry. I know how you feel about her. I—it's just that I care for her too," he said quietly.

She strained to hear their words. Damn. She wished she could see their faces.

"You *care* for her, but that's not *love* Jackson. I told you to always use a condom with her and I meant it," Jacob said angrily.

At his words, her eyes rounded as anger sprouted up inside her.

Stepping through the bedroom door, her eyes clashed with Jacob's furious gaze.

"You are such a bully. You've forced the rest of them to use protection, when you never do, even though we all agreed to it."

He visibly blanched at her words as a guilty look stole across his face, but she didn't back down.

"You're such a hypocrite! Out of all of them you're the main one who should have *always* used protection."

"What are you talking about?" Jacob gritted out.

"You have a girlfriend. I saw you with her."

"What the hell are you talking about?"

"Come up with another question, Jacob. You've already asked that one twice now."

"Jackson, we need some privacy," he clipped out tightly, his eyes never leaving her face.

She folded her arms across her chest. "This is my apartment, Jackson. You don't have to go anywhere."

"*Jackson.*" Jacob growled in warning.

"Stay!" She commanded.

She watched as Jackson stared back and forth between both of them as if he were refereeing a tennis match.

"Sorry, Camille. I think you two need to talk," he said quietly, before stepping between them to slip out of her apartment.

Her nostrils flared in anger.

"You're a bully."

Unfazed by her insults, Jacob held her gaze. "We need to talk."

She shook her head. "We have nothing to talk about, Jacob. If you're not here for sex then you can leave. The contract never said that I had to serve your conversational needs."

"Fuck that stupid contract. It's over — done! I should have never let this go on for so long anyway."

Fear settled in her gut. "You cannot terminate the contract now that my time is—"

His eyes softened a bit, although his body still vibrated with anger.

"I am not going back on my end of the deal. Your ranch belongs to you. It's yours," he said softly. He dragged a hand through his hair, before releasing a ragged breath. "I—I meant that you don't have to continue sleeping with my brothers any longer."

A vulnerable look crossed his face when he said those words and her mouth fell open at the raw emotion she glimpsed in his naked gaze. "I can't share you with them anymore, Camille. It's killing me to watch you with them and I just can't do it anymore. I nearly went to blows with Jackson twice when I got back from Houston and saw that you now favoured him—"

"I don't favour Jackson over you, Jacob. I just couldn't sleep with you when you got back from Houston because I discovered you had a girlfriend."

He shook his head, the anger creeping back into his eyes again. "You keep saying that, but it's not true. Who told you that?"

"No one. I saw you at *Chez Pierre's* with a stacked blonde when I was in Houston. I drew my own conclusions."

Sparks of fury leapt in his blue eyes as comprehension dawned on his face.

"But they were the *wrong* conclusions. That woman you saw me with is the daughter of an old family friend who passed away over a year ago. She sold her land to me earlier that day—land that has oil on it. Natalie lives in Chicago with her *fiancé*. She has no desire to move back to Texas which is why she wanted to get rid of her land. I took her out to dinner as a *friend* to celebrate the deal."

She closed her eyes, as her face heated with humiliation. *God, I was so stupid and insecure.*

"Yes, Camille. You've punished me for the past month for something I didn't do. After all the time we've spent together you should know that I would never make love to you, without protection no less, and then take another woman to my bed."

"I—I'm sorry, Jacob," she stammered quietly.

"That's not good enough," he whispered.

Her eyes snapped to his face.

"Per our agreement, you owe me one month."

"But you just released me from my contract."

A smile lit up Jacob's face as his expression became tender. Lifting his hand, he slowly caressed her cheek.

"I did, and now I'm just hoping that you would be willing to accept a *new* agreement."

She arched a single brow, now curious. She nodded. "Go on."

"You owe me one month, as my exclusive mistress. No brothers—just us." His hand stopped stroking her cheek so that he could lift her chin with his fingers.

A grin spread across her face. She enjoyed being with his brothers but the thought of being with *just* Jacob excited her. "I *do* owe you a month, don't I, but will your brothers be all right with this?"

His eyes flashed with what could only be described as possessiveness. "They all care about you, but not the way I do, and I think you know this."

She nodded because she did. From day one, she and Jacob had shared a more intimate relationship, but she'd been afraid to read more into it.

"They will accept that you are mine exclusively, because they know how I feel about you and they respect my feelings," he whispered as he dragged her into his embrace and held her close while he stroked his hand through her hair. "Camille, over the next month I really want us to begin to deal with our pasts and work to move forward. Do you think you can do that?"

She lifted her head from his chest and nodded. "I can do that."

"And you're okay with being just *my* mistress. You understand my brothers can no—"

She placed a single finger against his lips to halt his next words.

"I don't want any other man but you," she whispered firmly.

Glimpsing the truth of her words in her eyes, he seemed to visibly relax. She couldn't believe he'd truly worried that she wouldn't be able to let the rest of them go, but the vulnerable look in his gaze was unmistakable. It was clear he was still uncertain of the depth of her feelings for him. Well, she would just have to show him just how much he truly meant to her—starting now.

She lifted up on her tiptoes to claim his lips in a light, teasing kiss as her arms wound around his neck. He quickly caught on and hoisted her into his arms to carry her into her bedroom where for the rest of the night she did her best to show him that while she'd enjoyed her time with all the Downing brothers, there was only *one* Downing man for her.

A REBOUND AFFAIR

Dedication

To all my wonderful and loyal readers.

Chapter One

"I think I'm in love with your wife."

Jackson Downing stood ramrod straight, and steeled himself for the blow he knew would come. He deserved to be pummelled by Jacob and they both knew it. His brother had warned him that his attraction to Camille was more than *just* attraction. But he'd sworn to Jacob he was over her, that he'd accepted their marriage and was moving on, but he had lied. He was certain Jacob had known he'd lied, but his brother had said nothing at the time.

A tense silence permeated the room as they regarded each other warily. He had to admit he was a little surprised Jacob hadn't launched over the desk and beat the shit out of him as soon as the words left his mouth. Jacob had inherited the infamous Irish temper of their maternal grandfather, more so than any of the Downing brothers. So, he took it as a good sign that since Jacob hadn't resorted to violence, he still might be open to talking this out.

"I know," was all Jacob said, his already harsh face giving away nothing as he sat behind his desk, his entire body rigid.

"I figured you knew, which is why I'm leaving."

Jacob sighed. "And I had a feeling you were going to say that." He stood up from his chair and Jackson met the identical dark sapphire gaze of his brother.

"I don't want you to go, but I know this has been hard for you."

Jacob had no idea. Watching the woman he'd spent the past seven months falling in love with walk down the aisle with the brother he was closest to, was more than hard—it was excruciating.

"I know you've been itching to get back down south to oversee the drilling project on Natalie's old land in Hockley but with the wedding it had to be pushed aside…"

"And now you want to go in my place."

Jackson shrugged. "It could take a while to get the pipe in place, months even. You're a newly wed and it just doesn't make sense for you to be gone for months away from Camille when I can go instead." He wanted to add that he *needed* this trip more than anyone else, but he didn't. They both knew how desperate he was to get away from Macon, Texas.

"It's going to be a tough job and you're going to have your hands full with a foreman who is pissed that we're the new owners. I haven't met him, but he hasn't returned any of my calls and our email exchanges have been less than polite—"

"I don't care. I'll deal with it." He knew Jacob wouldn't deny him this. Besides they were well aware that with his laidback attitude and easygoing demeanour, Jackson had always been better suited than any of his brothers in dealing with business conflicts and handling negotiations.

"Alright." Jacob nodded. "If you want to go then the job is yours."

Jackson released a drawn out breath. Separated by just two years, Jackson knew his brother well, and could tell from the strained expression on Jacob's face that he really didn't want him to go, at least not like this. But, they both knew he had to.

There was no way he could remain in Macon any longer. Being away and dealing with the distraction of getting the pipeline running would hopefully give him the time he needed to get over Camille.

It had all seemed so simple. For six months Camille would serve his sexual needs and those of his three brothers, and when her time was up they would all walk away. Then, Camille would get her ranch back when it was over. But at some point along the way, Jacob and Camille had raised the stakes by falling in love. It was just unfortunate that he'd fallen in love with her too. He didn't begrudge his brother or Camille for finding happiness with each other. But he would be lying if he didn't admit that he hadn't taken it so well when Camille chose his brother over him. That she'd fallen in love with his brother and not him.

One of the hardest things he'd ever had to do was to stand beside Jacob and watch as he said "I do" to Camille. Ever since that day he'd been distant and withdrawn from Jacob, and it pained him to think their relationship would never be the same ever again. That had been the deciding factor for him. He had to leave and at least *try* to move on for all their sakes. He'd lost Camille and if he didn't learn to get over her, he would lose his brother too.

He was determined to do everything in his power to not let that happen. He would head down to Hockley for a few months, lick his wounds and try to forget about Camille, his feelings for her and the fact that he'd fallen in love with his brother's wife.

* * * *

"Damn you, Natalie," BJ Parker muttered angrily, her gaze following the shiny black Mercedes as it made its way along the dirt road towards where she stood in front of the ranch house.

Her half-sister had some nerve selling Cottonmouth Ranch and leaving her to deal with the new owner—*alone*. They both agreed that in order to pay off their father's gambling debts they would have to sell the ranch, but that didn't mean she had to like it.

She'd been the foreman since graduating from college ten years ago and had always envisioned taking over when their dad retired. But that vision had faded when her father fell ill two years ago and she discovered he was living under a mountain of debt. She'd done all she could to keep Cottonmouth solvent, but it hadn't been enough. By the time she'd taken over, it was already too late.

After their father's death, she and Natalie quickly sold the ranch, settled with their dad's creditors and moved on. Well, at least that's how her older sister saw things. Natalie had always hated life on the ranch, and now she was pleasantly oblivious as she carried on with her lavish life in Chicago, far away from the family ranch, their small town of Hockley, and all the troubles that selling Cottonmouth hadn't erased. Troubles *she* still had to deal with—the main one being the arrogant and overbearing new owner who had just parked his gleaming, luxury car smack dab in front of her home.

His incessant emails and phone calls had rankled on her nerves, but she realised it was nothing compared to the ire she felt when he filed out of his car.

She was a tall woman, nearly six feet, and despite the distance she could tell he would tower over her. She hated that, but not quite as much as she hated how his thickly muscled frame rippled beneath his custom tailored black suit.

"Damn, pretty-boy, Jackson Downing," she found herself grumbling under her breath as he strolled towards her. She had never met him personally, but had seen the many covers of *Fortune* and *Money* with Jackson and his brothers placed front and centre. So, it was hard *not* to recognise the handsome ranch owner, even with his eyes hidden behind tinted aviator shades.

As he neared, she felt the hair on the back of her neck rise. She also knew she wore a surly frown across her face. She despised him and his brothers for buying her ranch, and the fact that she was now his employee. She wasn't a big fan of his flashy city-slicker demeanour either. Men like him didn't know a damn about hard work and the long days spent running a ranch. And if his emails were any evidence, she had no doubt he was going to bulldoze over her and the meticulous operation she ran just to assert his newfound authority and show everyone who was in charge.

"Good morning. I'm Jackson Downing, the new owner of Cottonmouth Ranch. I called last night to let the foreman know I was coming in today," he said as he came to a halt before her.

He extended his hand, flashing her a dimpled smile, but she didn't acknowledge either as she kept her arms folded across her breasts, her expression blank. She knew she was being rude, especially when he shot her a quizzical frown and let his hand fall back to his side, but she didn't care. As far as she was concerned, he was not welcome.

Several seconds ticked by, the air thick with tension, as they stood in silence. Finally, he cleared his throat in a somewhat futile attempt to ease the awkward moment.

"I wonder if you can help me. I'm looking for BJ Parker."

"And you just found her," she said stiffly, bracing herself for what she knew would come next. No matter how many times it happened, she always got a thrill watching the shock cross the faces of men expecting to meet, well—a *man*. And this time was no exception. Jackson Downing tugged his sunglasses from his face to stare down at her with questioning blue eyes, as if somehow the glasses had hidden the fact that she was, after all, a woman.

"You're BJ Parker? The foreman."

"That's me."

His brows knitted together as he frowned. "I...um was expecting—"

"A man?" she offered.

"No. I spoke with Natalie before I arrived. She told me her sister was the foreman. I knew you were a woman."

She smiled at the puzzled look on his face. He looked like a fish out of water. Most people did when they discovered her svelte, blonde sister, was in fact *her* sister.

"But I didn't expect you to be—"

"Black," she said with a slight shrug. "Natalie's my half-sister." Her lips curled into a tiny grin. "I guess you can tell which *half* we don't share."

She could say that again.

He swept his gaze over her, doing his best not to let his eyes linger. Yet even with his brief perusal of the woman known as BJ Parker he did not miss the subtle curves on her tall slender frame, carefully hidden behind a pair of well worn jeans and a baggy plaid shirt. He also didn't miss the exquisite beauty of her face, despite the Stetson that cast a dark shadow over her features. Even if she'd stood before him with a paper bag over her head he would have still been able to tell she was a natural beauty, a beauty that was rivalled only by her blatant animosity towards him.

He was surprised when a wave of heat inched across his skin, and he cleared his throat in an attempt to help clear his head. This woman was an endless parade of surprises. And from what little information he could pry out of Natalie on his drive there that morning, she was also going to be tough to win over. Whatever interest his body had in her would have to be ignored because he was there to do business, and nothing more.

"Well, I'm glad to finally meet you," he said with a curt nod. He almost extended his hand again, but then quickly remembered she hadn't been too keen on shaking his hand the first time. Apparently, she also wasn't too keen on meeting him since she didn't offer a similar reply, the lovely features of her face as stoic as a blank mask.

He let out an inward sigh. This was going to be a long trip if she didn't lose the attitude, but he didn't have the energy to deal with her or her surly disposition right now. He could confront her later. Right now all he wanted to do was unpack and settle in after the five-hour drive south.

He spun away from her, popped the trunk and dug out two large black suitcases. As soon as he moved towards her, he noticed her entire demeanour had changed. She went from being just slightly rude to openly hostile, as she stood before the two steps leading up to the house, her stance wide with her arms still folded tightly across her chest. She looked like a bouncer guarding the entrance to an exclusive nightclub in Manhattan. It would have been laughable had he not been so exhausted and eager to get to his room where he could unwind.

"What are you doing?"

"I'm taking my things inside so that I can relax before we talk business." He stepped to the side, but she shifted in that direction to block his path.

"I don't think so, Mr. Downing. This is my home and you weren't invited."

"Not according to Natalie. She said I could stay here for as long as I liked, so that's what I'm doing."

Angry red flames flared to life in her topaz gaze, and he knew instantly that those were the last words she wanted to hear.

"Well, Natalie doesn't live here. I do. And as the foreman, I decide who comes and goes on this property."

His eyes hardened, and he levelled her with a steely glare, causing her to take a tiny step back. From the wary expression on her face, she must have quickly realised he was not to be trifled with. But, just in case she wasn't too sure, his next words made it absolutely clear that he would not be pushed around by her.

"You don't get to make the decisions around here anymore, BJ, because as of right now, *you're fired.*"

"What?"

He almost pitied BJ Parker, who stood there with her mouth agape and her eyes wide. He was sure she hadn't been expecting that. And truth be told, he hadn't really wanted to throw down the gauntlet in such a high handed manner. He needed this woman because she knew the land better than anyone else. But from what he knew of her, and what he'd just witnessed, she was not used to people challenging her nor was she used to taking orders, and he couldn't stand for that. The Downing brothers were now the new owners of Cottonmouth, and she would either have to accept that and learn to work with him or she could find herself a new job.

"This is *my* home," she gritted out angrily.

Her caramel hued cheeks glowed red with fury, and despite the rage pouring off of her in waves, he still found himself feeling a twinge of guilt as he glimpsed the pain in her eyes. Unlike her sister, he could tell this place meant something to her and for some inexplicable reason he knew that tearing her from her land would be like tearing out her soul. He empathised with her, but didn't cave under the weight of her fury. This was business and if she couldn't do her job then she couldn't stay.

"You cannot kick me out of my home and off my land."

"Let's get this one thing straight—by law I *can*, but I don't *want* to and that's certainly not why I came here. I came here to get the pipeline up and running in order to funnel out oil, but if you're determined to make things difficult for me then I will have no choice but to fire you."

"You won't find oil without me," she said stiffly, her eyes as hard and cold as granite.

Something about the way she said those words had him seeing red. He was a man slow to anger so the very fact he felt heat crawling along the back of his neck was not a good sign for either of them.

Still holding his bags, he closed the distance between them so that she was forced to crane her head back in order to meet his ferocious gaze.

"I don't tend to do well with threats or blackmail so if you have plans to sabotage this operation you won't have to worry about getting fired because I'll have your ass thrown in jail."

She snorted, seemingly unmoved by his threat, which was surprising. Most people caved under the weight of his fury.

"I won't have to lift a finger to sabotage you because as soon as you send me away you'll be hard pressed to locate even a single drop of oil. And don't think Natalie can help you. She hasn't spent more than a night here since she was eighteen. You can fire me, *city-boy* but then be prepared to comb over more than a hundred acres looking for what I could find with my eyes closed."

The smug look on her face annoyed the hell out of him, but it was the way she called him a *city-boy* that really pissed him off. She probably thought because he wore a suit and drove a fancy car that he would prove himself to be a walking moron if left out in the wide open space of the Texas plains. But she was wrong. All of his brothers spent their days working out on the ranch. Even Jacob spent a fair amount of time doing ranch work, despite the fact that he was the main one who ran the business end. If this woman thought he was a spoilt and pampered rich playboy then she was in for a surprise.

"I don't care if you can find oil in your sleep. If you can't find a way to cooperate with me then I will have no choice but to let you go."

If looks could kill, he would have been dead as soon as he stepped out of his car, but the glare she shot him now was a thousand times worse. He half expected to go up in flames at any moment from the look in her eyes, which was damn near incendiary.

"I can cooperate as long as you understand that I'm in charge," she finally bit out, and he knew it must have pained her to say even that.

"I have no interest in running your ranch. My only reason for being here is to set up drilling operations. That's it," he said, although he itched to remind her that she was *not* in charge, at least not entirely, but he wasn't one to look a gift horse in the mouth. She was willing to cooperate, which meant he could finally unpack his things, and get some rest. He could deal with the semantics of their arrangement later, when he was well rested.

She continued to stand there for a long moment, still rooted in the same spot, and he wondered wearily if she was going to force him to fire her for real this time. Luckily, she just shrugged and turned away from him.

"I'll show you to the guest room," she called from over her shoulder, her long braid whipping down her back. Jackson didn't miss her less than enthused expression before turning her back to him, or the deadpan tone of her voice. Even if he had, the rigid lines of her slender back would have given her away as she disappeared inside the house on long, stiff legs.

He slipped inside to follow after her, all the while mentally preparing himself for the hard reality that the next several months were going to be hell.

It was a sad irony. BJ was as beautiful as a desert rose, but about as pleasant as a cactus, and he had no doubt she would prove to be a thorn in his side the entire time.

Chapter Two

"What are you saying?" BJ could feel heat rising along the back of her neck. The mid-morning Texas sun beat down on her, but that had nothing to do with her skyrocketing temperature.

"I'm sorry, BJ," the man said with a shrug.

BJ glared at Dwight McDonnell. *He* was sorry? She'd show him sorry.

"You're sorry? No, I'm sorry. How the hell am I going to run this place without water?"

Dwight had the good sense to at least appear remorseful. She tried to rein in her anger. It wasn't his fault. He was only doing his job. Cottonmouth rented well water from the neighbouring ranch, McDonnell Hill, but with their debts and mounting bills, she'd put off paying the McDonnell's for three months. She knew if she didn't pay today Cottonmouth would have to find another water supply.

"Can you at least give me a few more days?"

"I'm sorry, BJ but every month you keep telling me to give you a few more days." He sighed. "I'm *really* sorry."

BJ started to beg again, but stopped when the screen door banged shut. Jackson sauntered down the front porch steps as if he owned the place. She twisted her lips into a surly frown. Well, technically he did own the place.

"Good morning. What seems to be the problem?"

"Who says there's a problem?" She shot Dwight a hard look, the expression on her face indicating she wanted him to keep his mouth shut. She didn't need Jackson Downing sweeping in there to save her family home. She could take care of this all by herself.

"Jackson Downing," he said extending his hand to Dwight for a brief shake. "I'm the new owner. Is there something I can help you with?"

Dwight glanced between her and Jackson, before apparently deciding Jackson was his ticket to getting paid. "W—well if you're the new owner then yes, there is." She glared at Dwight, but that didn't stop him from telling Jackson she was behind on the well rent.

When he was done, Jackson simply nodded his head in the direction of the house. "If you come inside I can write you a cheque."

BJ stood there fuming as they walked off, leaving her standing alone, glaring at their backs. It was so easy for him. Just write a cheque and be done with it. She worked hard to keep this place going and he simply walked right in as if nothing was too big or tough to handle.

She stomped off towards the stables, but drew up short when she heard her name.

"Why didn't you tell me about the water?"

She spun around, levelling Jackson with a stern glare. "Because I was handling it."

His expression was incredulous. "You were handling it? How? You were three months behind. What else have you forgotten to tell me?"

"I haven't *forgotten* to tell you anything."

He marched towards her, his sapphire eyes flashing with red sparks. She gasped when he gripped her by the arms, pinning her against his body.

"Let's get this straight, BJ. If I wake up tomorrow and find anything from the electricity to the cable cut off, you're fired."

What was with him and always threatening to fire her? "We don't have cable."

His eyes hardened. "This is a joke to you. You think if you keep me in the dark long enough and frustrate me to no end I will give up and walk away."

That's exactly what she'd thought, but she had the feeling that Jackson Downing wouldn't be as easy to get rid of as she hoped. He'd already lasted two weeks, and she'd been trying her damnedest. But, if there was ever any doubt that Jackson was made of sterner stuff, his next words erased it.

"I'm not walking away, BJ so you can end this war right here and right now. Even if I did leave, I would only send another one of my brothers here to take my place. Either way you're stuck with a new owner, so get used to it."

"I don't want to get used to it. I want you to go away."

"You sound like a child. And besides we talked about this when I first got here. If you can't get over this then you need to leave."

She couldn't believe he had called her childish. Her temper flared again. Maybe she should quit. Maybe she should just walk away and find a job elsewhere, because she seriously doubted that she and Jackson would ever manage to see eye-to-eye on anything.

For the first time she realised he still held her by the arms, with her body pressed against his hard chest. She tried to pull free of his grasp, but he only gripped her tighter, reminding her that Jackson was a very strong, very *virile* man. A warm flush spread over her, heating her skin, and despite her best effort not to, she shivered.

She fought to mask her surprise, and deftly avoided his gaze, but she could not escape the weight of his stare. She refused to look at him, she couldn't do it—not right now, not after her body had just reacted to him. She wasn't attracted to him. Couldn't be. She could barely stand his guts.

"I need to get back to work," she said, her voice unsteady. She wondered if he noticed.

"Do you think you can push it back to this afternoon? The reason why I came out here in the first place was to invite you to lunch."

Her head snapped up, and before she could stop herself, she blurted out, "What?"

"Lunch? It's that meal humans eat in the middle of the day." His lips furled into a crooked grin, and a tiny dimple winked at her. Her stomach did a flip-flop, and she shivered again. What the hell was wrong with her?

"I know what lunch is, smart ass." She jerked against him again, and this time he let her go. "I guess my question is what for? Why are you inviting *me* to lunch?"

"Besides the fact that we both have to eat?" He shrugged. "I would like for us to sit down and talk. I'm hoping you can get me up to speed on this place, and lunch seemed as good a time as any—especially since you seem to be so busy practically every hour of the day..."

His voice trailed off, a pointed reference to how she'd been purposely dodging his attempts to talk to her about the ranch. She started to refuse, as she'd done many times before, but when he smiled again she finally understood why he'd been voted one of *People* magazine's "Sexiest Men Alive". It was that damn dimple. Women probably threw their panties at him when he walked down the street. Hell, she was thinking about tossing her own, even though she knew he wouldn't want them.

He was only trying to charm her in order to get her to go to lunch, where he would just pry information out of her, so that he could do her job for her. No, thanks.

"I have a lot of work to do."

"It's only lunch, Bria," he said softly as if he were tiptoeing around a rattle snake.

Her name on his lips made everything inside her freeze. The only person who'd ever called her Bria had been her mother. BJ had always thought it was far too pretty of a name for a girl like her, hence, BJ. But when Jackson said it, it actually sounded quite nice.

"It's just a lunch so we can talk about how to keep Cottonmouth afloat. I'm sure you want that as much as I do."

She sighed. He knew he had her. She lived for this place. She would do anything to see that it didn't fall into the red again. Besides, she couldn't avoid him forever, and it was apparent he'd caught on to her dodging act.

"Fine. Let me just grab a few things and I'll meet you back here in ten minutes."

* * * *

Lunch turned out to be quite interesting.

BJ had complained from the moment they set foot in the fine dining Italian restaurant.

She was underdressed.

They should have gone to a regular place.

She really wasn't a big fan of Italian food.

Jackson sat there, carefully hiding his smile. She was nervous and felt out of place, and he didn't know why, but he found that endearing. BJ wasn't as tough as she pretended to be.

It felt good to see that *Ms. Thorny Rose* was human just like everyone else.

And after she got past her nerves, lunch went smoothly. He'd been surprised. They actually had a lot in common, and the conversation flowed so easily that it wasn't until they were leaving that he realised he'd hardly asked any of the questions about the ranch that he'd wanted to.

Next time.

Next time?

He made it out to be like they'd gone out on some sort of date, and now he was actually looking forward to doing it again.

He froze.

He glanced over at her, his lips pursed into a frown. He wasn't there to get to know her. He was there to get information out of her.

Unease washed over him when he realised what was happening. He didn't want to notice her as a woman *or* be attracted to her, but that didn't erase the fact that he was. He was intrigued by her—the toughest talking woman he'd ever met, with one of the prettiest faces he'd ever seen. She was a wondrous study of contrasts and there were times when he caught himself looking at her, when she wasn't aware of his presence.

He cursed inwardly, his attraction to her catching him by surprise because she wasn't even his type. For starters, she was tall. The top of her head would touch his chin if they stood facing each other. She was too tall, too edgy, with too much attitude. There was no denying that she was all woman, but he liked his women softer, rounder, more voluptuous. She was rail thin. His eyes dipped to her chest. All right, not *that* thin, but her breasts would barely fill his palm, if that.

His cock hardened. Apparently it didn't care how big or small her breasts were. He shifted uncomfortably, trying to ease the tightness in his pants. He had no business thinking about BJ's breasts, or any other part of her anatomy for that matter.

"What's wrong with you?"

She stared at him with curious eyes, her brow furrowed. He realised then that he'd abruptly stopped in the middle of the sidewalk. She must have thought he was nuts.

"Nothing," he said, lightly grabbing her elbow. "We better get back."

He ushered her towards the parking lot, but stopped at the sound of a voice calling her name from behind them.

They spun around, at the same time the man shouting her name caught up with them.

"Lou. Hi."

Jackson frowned when she stepped away from him to embrace Lou in a hug that went on far too long for it to just be a friendly gesture.

When she finally managed to disentangle herself, she introduced them, but by then Jackson barely heard her. He couldn't even be certain he mumbled anything in return that would be considered polite.

His gaze remained glued to the young man who stood there with stars in his eyes, staring down at BJ. Jackson took an instant disliking to him. There was just something about Lou that made Jackson want to draw BJ under his arm and shield her from the guy.

"We better get going, Lou," BJ said after a few minutes. "It was nice running into you."

Jackson didn't feel the same so he simply nodded. The vibes he got from Lou didn't sit right with him. The man was eager—a little *too* eager.

"That was rude of you," BJ said as soon as he slid behind the steering wheel.

"What was rude of me?"

"The way you treated Lou. You barely said three words to him."

He'd said three. That was three more than he'd wanted to. "So? How was I rude? I spoke, didn't I?"

Her eyes widened, her golden pupils darkening to the colour of aged whisky. "Is that how you city boys treat people? You think you're so much better than the rest of us that you can just ignore everyone around you?"

"City boy?" His brows lifted. "I was raised in Macon! It's smaller than Hockley, which is basically a glorified suburb of Houston." He couldn't believe he was trading insults with her on where they'd grown up. He turned on the car, his entire body vibrating with anger.

"Besides, if you hadn't been so busy sucking up compliments from your lapdog, you would have realised Lou is nothing but a phony—"

"A phony?" She folded her arms across her chest. "How so?"

"He's a gold-digger."

He gritted his teeth at the husky laughter that floated around him. She had a beautiful laugh, but it grated on his ears at that particular moment.

"How could Lou possibly be digging for gold? If you haven't noticed, I'm practically broke, and Cottonmouth would have gone under had you not come along. He should have been sucking up to *you* if he was a smart gold-digger."

Jackson frowned. She was smart—she had to be to run a ranch like Cottonmouth on her own. So, why was she being so thick-headed?

"Trust me, Bria. He's a gold-digger. There's oil on your land, and as soon as I find it, you will be a rich woman." She had her sister, Natalie to thank for that. Natalie may have sold their land, but not future rights to oil and gold profits. Natalie and Bria would only receive a small percentage, but if his hunch was right, that small percentage was worth at least six figures.

"So the only man that would ever want me has to be after my money. Is that it?"

She turned away from him, and he realised too late that he'd stuck his foot in his mouth. He hadn't meant to hurt her feelings, but he was telling the truth. Lou had dollar signs in his eyes when he looked at her. The man was no good.

"Don't go putting words in my mouth. You know every man that wants you isn't after your money, but Lou is."

The withering look she shot him told him his last statement hadn't made things better.

She was beautiful. Men were probably beating down her door—well, if they could get past that acid tongue of hers. She had to know that most men were not after her for money, not with everything she had to offer.

He glanced over at her again. Her face was practically glued to the window, her body rigid. For her to say what she had—to immediately jump to the conclusion that a man wouldn't want her unless she came with money, made him think that maybe she didn't realise just how special she was. Maybe she had no idea how utterly captivating she was, and that even after only two weeks, and despite her animosity towards him, he found himself drawn to her, to the point that he had to tell himself—and his body to leave her alone.

He shook his head, and turned his attention back to the road. He'd taken her out to lunch to soften her up, but like the idiot he was, he'd insulted her, and now she was back to being cold as ice.

Maybe that was for the best. He found himself attracted to BJ, but he really didn't need to get entangled with a woman, especially *this* woman, not after everything he'd been through.

BJ was a complication he could ill afford.

* * * *

Just when she had started to think they could get along...

Lunch had turned out surprisingly well. He was funny, witty, charming—even nice. But as soon as they set foot in his car, the real Jackson had re-emerged yet again.

BJ should have known they weren't meant to be anything remotely resembling friends. He was a moron, an idiot, a complete asshole.

So she wasn't pretty—all right, she got it. He didn't have to rub it in by pointing out that she had to be draped in dollar bills for a man to notice her.

She took a sip of wine and closed her eyes. See, what he had done? In just two weeks, he'd driven her to drink!

Her eyelids snapped open at the sound of hushed footsteps along the staircase.

He was up. She jumped out of her chair and dumped her glass of wine down the sink, trying to make a hasty exit out of the kitchen before he made it down the stairs, but she wasn't fast enough.

She collided into him, just as he was entering the kitchen. The solid wall of his chest forced the air out of her lungs and he gripped her arms to keep her from falling backwards.

Damn it. Even in the middle of the night she couldn't seem to escape him.

"What are you doing up so late?" He scowled down at her.

"I could say the same to you. I couldn't sleep."

His face softened. "Me either."

Something flashed in his gaze that made her wonder what it was that kept his nights sleepless, but she refused to ask. It was none of her business.

He leant towards her and sniffed the air. "Were you drinking?"

"Wine."

He arched a brow. "Can I have some?"

She looked at him again, seeing him clearly for the first time. He looked haggard, his eyes haunted. She felt herself softening towards him just a bit. Whatever had kept him up weighed heavily on him. If anyone needed a drink, it was him.

"Sit down. I'll get it."

She reached for the red wine under the counter, and filled two wine glasses.

Handing him one, she sat down across from him, and took a sip.

Silence stretched between them as they drank, both retreating to the dark corners of their minds. She itched to ask him why he was still up, but she tempered her curiosity. He didn't seem like he was in the mood for questions, and neither was she.

"I'm sorry about what I said earlier."

She stared at him. She hadn't been expecting him to acknowledge what had happened at lunch, let alone an apology, so she sat there speechless.

"As pretty as you are, I'm sure you get plenty of interest from men and, in turn, are interested in many of them right back. It was just that with your friend earlier, I could tell he was all wrong for you, but if you like him," he shrugged, "I don't think he's a good guy, but if you like him then that's your business, not mine. I shouldn't have interfered."

She sort of heard everything he said, but she really couldn't get past the part where he'd called her pretty. Her. Bria Jaslene 'BJ' Parker? Jackson Downing had called her pretty, and he seemed to believe it. She looked away because she didn't want him to see the disbelief in her eyes.

The only reason why he thought she was pretty was because he obviously hadn't met her sister, or seen a picture of her mother. Those two were pretty, *no* gorgeous. Now, her? Well, she was a different story. She had always been too tall, too skinny, her features too angular, her actions too rough. Next to her mother and Natalie, she'd never been girly, or feminine, or even passably pretty.

Jackson noticed the change in her the moment he started to apologise. She didn't look at him, and the entire room grew chilly, as if the temperature had dipped twenty degrees.

She abruptly shot to her feet and the chair scraped against the floor, nearly tumbling over.

"Where are you going?"

"Back to bed."

He grabbed her arm before she could scurry out of there.

"What's wrong with you? I thought you would appreciate my apology." He didn't mean to raise his voice, but he had apologised and she hadn't so much as said a word. He was trying here, but she had to at least meet him halfway.

"I do appreciate your apology. Thank you. I'm just tired. I better get to bed now."

He narrowed his gaze. She was lying. She couldn't even look him in the eye. What was up with her? One minute she was hot, the next she was cold. What had he said to set her off this time?

If there was one thing he knew, he knew women. He searched his brain, trying to piece together the mystery that was BJ Parker, but when he settled on an explanation it was so baffling he swore he had to be wrong. And yet, it was the only thing that made sense.

"So is Lou your boyfriend or something?" He asked tentatively, testing the waters. If he knew nothing else, he knew that with BJ blunt questions would get him nowhere.

"What does that have to do with me going to bed?"

"Nothing. It's just that you seemed upset when I mentioned him just now. I thought I offended you because he's your boyfriend."

Her eyes darkened and he wondered if she would even answer him. Then, she said softly, "No, Lou's not my boyfriend."

"Good. You deserve better Bria. You're far too lovely..."

She stiffened, and he knew his hunch, as absurd as it seemed, was right.

He still held her by the arm, but he reached for her with his free hand, when she tried to pull away, the look in her eyes as blank and empty as a cloudless sky.

"Bria—"

"Good night, Jackson."

She struggled to wrench herself free, but he trapped her between his body and the refrigerator.

He didn't want to embarrass her by pressing the issue, but he found it hard to believe that she didn't see herself the way he did—the way he knew other men did as well.

He pressed his lower body against her, making words unnecessary at that point, there was no need for declarations with the evidence of his arousal right there.

She gasped, her eyes wide, as if she couldn't believe that he was aroused by her, that he wanted her. Damn it, he wanted her. He'd tossed and turned practically every night thinking about her. This was undoubtedly the tenth night she'd haunted his dreams, and hell, he'd only been there two fucking weeks.

He'd been in a painful state of arousal from the moment he walked into the kitchen and found her there, dressed in a poor excuse for a night shirt. The practically sheer white cotton moulded to her subtle curves, the moonlight outlining every dip and valley.

He dipped his head to inhale her scent and she shivered against him. That was the last thing she should have done. His body grew tighter, all blood leaving his brain and flowing straight to his cock.

He leant into her and when she lifted her head, he took that as a sign. He brushed his lips against hers, giving her one last chance to push him away. When her tongue darted out to sweep across his lips, he groaned low in his throat, crushing his mouth to hers. He plundered inside with his tongue, tasting her, coaxing tiny moans of pleasure from her full lips.

He rocked against her, his cock grinding into her belly. Every inch of him was on fire and all he could think about was freeing his aching shaft and sliding into her wet heat.

Pressing his body closer, he skimmed his hand down the length of her leg. Her skin was smooth, the silky slide making his body grow harder with need. His questing hand caused her shirt to hitch higher up her thighs, and he slipped his fingers between her legs, a deep, guttural growl escaping his lips when he found nothing but the hot wet heat of her.

He lifted his head, and grinned. "No panties, Bria?" His hardnosed foreman wasn't as uptight as he'd first assumed.

Her eyes widened, her cheeks blooming red with embarrassment and he crushed his lips to hers again, claiming her sweet lips in a searing kiss. He pushed inside her with his fingers, stroking deep, the warm slide of her pussy causing violent tremors to rack him as he fought for control.

She writhed against him and her breasts grazed his chest. He pumped inside her tight sheath, harder and faster. When he rubbed the tiny nub at the mouth of her cunt, she nearly came undone, her body quivering.

He waged his assault on her body with his lips, his hands, until she splintered in his arms, coming on his still thrusting fingers, her groan of pleasure flowing from her mouth to his. She was so wet, so sticky, and the sweet musk of her cum filled the room.

He pulled away from her, ending their kiss, and a small smile curled his lips at her puffy, bee stung mouth. He leant into her, a sigh escaping him. He ached to sheath himself in her pulsing heat, to hear the soft cry of his name on her lips as he fucked her to climax after climax.

He'd never been this consumed by need for a woman before, this complete obsession to claim her. The only other time he'd come close to feeling this way had been when he'd been with Camille.

He stilled, abruptly jerking away from BJ.

Camille.

He stared down at the woman before him. She was *nothing* like Camille, or the women he was normally attracted to, and yet, he wanted her with such a burning passion that he hadn't been able to sleep all night.

He eased away from her. No matter how much he wanted her, he couldn't make love to BJ, not tonight, not with his body and mind so conflicted. He was there to do a job, and had come there in order to get over Camille. The last thing he needed was a rebound affair, and BJ certainly deserved better than that.

"I'm sorry. I shouldn't have done that." He knew it was lame, but he gave her a curt nod anyway, because he didn't know what else to do.

"Good night," he said weakly and walked out of there before he changed his mind and took her right there up against the refrigerator—something he knew he would only regret later.

Chapter Three

BJ was already up and preparing to cook breakfast by the time Jackson strolled into the kitchen. She hadn't been able to sleep, their lovemaking from the night before had left her tossing and turning. It had all been so unexpected, and then ended so abruptly. She still wasn't sure how she felt about everything. There was no denying Jackson was an attractive man, but she didn't need, nor *want*, to get entangled with him. She was a small town girl, who hadn't had sex in so long that she'd stopped counting the months. He was cosmopolitan and refined. If the society pages were to be believed, international super models graced his bed on a regular basis. She looked down at her well-worn jeans and faded work shirt. Yeah, she was going to give Heidi Klum a run for her money one of these days.

Footsteps echoed along the staircase and she glanced up just as Jackson barrelled into the kitchen. She bit back a slight grimace when her stomach did a tiny flip-flop at the sight of him. Hadn't she just decided that she didn't need to get involved with him? Her body must not have heard, because it hummed to life at the sight of him dressed in a pair of snug fitting jeans and a plaid shirt that stretched across his muscled chest. The sleeves were rolled up, revealing bronzed forearms covered in a smattering of hair. He was ruggedly sexy, and she shifted on her feet, fighting to ignore the sticky wetness that gathered between her thighs.

Their gazes met, as she swallowed the hard lump in her throat at the look in his sapphire eyes. He knew she was checking him out, but there wasn't a bit of smugness on his face. Instead, a spark of desire burned in his eyes, making her hot all over.

She turned away before he could glimpse the warm blush creeping into her cheeks.

"I was just about to cook breakfast. Do you want some?" She asked nervously, trying to ease the sexual tension in the small kitchen.

"What are you making?" The deep bass of his voice vibrated from behind her, so close that she could feel the slight ripple along her back.

"Eggs, bacon and some toast." She leant away from him, as the smell of his cologne tickled her nose. When he was near, her body grew warm in places she didn't want to think about.

"You want some?" She asked again.

"Sure." He took a seat in the chair across from her, a grin on his face. "So you can cook too? What other hidden talents do you have that I don't know about?"

The question was innocent enough, but the way he said it and the twinkle in his eyes charged it with a sexual energy that made every inch of her body go from warm to scorching.

"I have many, *many* talents, Jackson Downing. You have no idea," she said teasingly, trying to lighten the mood.

"So I've noticed." She pretended not to see his gaze as it lingered on her lips and then her breasts, before inching its way back to her face.

So much for lightening the mood. She turned her attention back to the frying pan and tried to ignore the aching peaks of her nipples that pushed against her bra. She was so out of her element with Jackson. His notion of flirting was potent, lethal even.

"What's on your agenda today?" She asked, trying to steer their conversation back to neutral waters, giving her body time to recover.

"Was going to ride out and survey the land." He arched a brow. "Are you busy today?"

She knew what he was really asking of her, but she played dumb. "I'm always busy. I'm the foreman, remember?"

He stood up. "And that's why I believe you have a good idea where it is I should start looking for oil." His gaze bore into her while she busied herself with dishing eggs onto their plates. She ignored him.

He was there to find oil, and they both knew he needed her help. Even so, she still hadn't gotten over the fact that this was her land—not his. He didn't belong there.

"You've lived here all your life."

He was hedging. "So." She reached around him to set his plate of food on the table. "Orange juice is in the fridge."

He sidestepped her, blocking her path. "I'm not the enemy, Bria. If I find oil, you stand to make money too."

She pursed her lips into a tight line. "If you find oil? You shouldn't even be here. This is my father's land, my father's ranch. Any oil you find should belong to my family, not you."

"I've gone over your books dozens of times." His expression was harsh as he closed the distance between them. "And you're delusional if you think you would have ever been able to find oil on this land without *some* outside help. Drilling operations are expensive and let's be honest, you would never have been able to raise the capital to afford that type of equipment."

She knew that much, but he just didn't get it. "I don't care about the oil. I never have. All I care about is that this ranch stays in my family."

His eyes softened, but he didn't say a word. What could he say? They both knew he wasn't giving her the ranch back, and that was all she wanted.

"Thanks for breakfast." He said with resignation in his eyes, although, she could tell he wanted to push, yet, he didn't. Instead, he gathered up his plate and started to leave the kitchen then, but she stopped him with a light touch to his arm.

"Wait." She drew in a deep breath. She didn't want to help him, but he was right. He *wasn't* the enemy. He had simply bought a ranch that her sister had sold and they never would have been in that position had it not been for their father in the first place.

Jackson could have stormed in there, fired everyone—including her—and replaced them with his own people, but he hadn't. He was there to find oil, and only oil. The ranching operation he'd left to her. Those were the actions of a good person, a good man. The least she could do was repay his sense of fairness.

"I'll have some free time in the afternoon. Why don't you meet me at the stables?"

He nodded, a small smile creeping across his face, causing her stomach to do another flip. She let out an inward groan at the adorable dimple that peeked out from his cheek. She was supposed to be maintaining a polite distance, not helping him, and certainly not melting into a mass of jelly at his feet. But here she was, softening towards him—and all for what? A cute dimple and sexy smile? She shook her head.

That's just pathetic, BJ. You could've at least made him work for it.

* * * *

BJ knew she'd caved in too easily that morning, but she didn't feel so bad about it when she made it to the stables and caught a glimpse of Jackson Downing trying to saddle up her prized stallion, Bolt.

She grinned as she moved towards them, nearly bursting with laughter when the skittish black stallion refused to let Jackson mount him and instead dumped him right on his ass.

"What's wrong with him? You told me he was broken in." Jackson growled at her stable boy, Riley.

"He is," BJ said with a smirk. "He just doesn't seem to like city slicker boys." She ran her hand across Bolt's shiny black coat, and he neighed softly, inching his way towards her.

"I'll take it from here, Riley," she said, dismissing him. She could mount Bolt without any help. She glanced over at Jackson who was dusting off his jeans—now he was a different story.

He definitely needs help, she thought, with an inward grin.

"You want to take out something more docile, maybe one of our ponies?"

"You think this is funny?"

She giggled, "I think this is hilarious. Jackson Downing can't even mount a little colt."

"He's not a colt." Jackson glared at her. "He's fully grown and despite what you and your stable boy say, he's not trained. I know you set me up on purpose."

She launched herself onto Bolt's back, all the while keeping her eyes locked with Jackson's. A smug smile crossed her face when the stallion didn't so much as move a muscle.

"Bolt's as timid as a mouse, if the rider knows what he *or she* is doing." She grabbed the reins. "I'll wait while you grab a pony."

He nailed her with his ice blue eyes. "I'm getting one of your geldings. Maybe you took the time to train one of them."

She didn't even bat and eye at his insult. "Ahhh, so we're giving up on the stallions, I see," she called after him when he disappeared into one of the stalls. "Not man enough?"

Her comment was met with silence. Minutes later, he returned sitting astride her favourite mare, Bluebell.

"Hey! That's my horse." She frowned at him, and at Bluebell—the traitor who was just as happy and content as could be. Bluebell and Bolt were siblings and shared a skittish and wild tempered nature. No one but BJ had ever been able to ride either of them—until now.

"Bluebell's yours? I didn't know."

Liar. He'd seen her ride Bluebell twice.

She ignored him and trotted away from the stables, stopping just at the edge of the fence to glance over her shoulder, a small smile on her face.

"Bluebell's quite a handful. Let's see if the famous Downing charm works on *any* species."

She turned around and took off on Bolt, but not before Jackson shot back. "I haven't met one female I couldn't handle — " BJ couldn't quite make out Jackson's last words over the roar of Bolt's hoof beats, but she swore she heard him say, *"including you. "*

They'd see about that.

* * * *

"This is the last spot," BJ remarked as Jackson dismounted beside her.

They'd been riding all afternoon and his shirt clung to him as sweat trickled down his chest and back. His muscles would ache in the morning, but he didn't care.

It was nice to get out and ride every now and then. He hadn't done it in awhile.

He stood beside her, surveying the land before him. Rugged, desert terrain stretched for miles and miles around him in every direction. Most people would see nothing but barren earth, but Jackson knew that rivers of oil flowed just beneath the surface—they just had to find it.

He turned to face her. "Out of all three of the places we've been to, which one do you think is the best spot?" He had a hunch, but wanted to get her input as well.

She glanced over at him, the light catching her topaz eyes, that were shadowed by the broad brim of her Stetson. He was so mesmerised by their golden depths that it took him a second to realise she was speaking.

"Truthfully, I believe all three have oil beneath them, but I think you'll have the best chance of finding oil here without having to shell out a great deal of money."

"Really? Why?"

She stared straight ahead, her gaze fixed on the sun setting in the distance. "Most of it's a hunch, but there are times when I come out here and swear I can feel the earth move beneath my feet." She turned her honey brown eyes on him. "I know there's oil down there. I can just feel it."

And he believed her. She knew this land as intimately as she would know her lover's body. BJ's heart and soul were tied to Cottonmouth, it was there in her eyes. She was passionate about her ranch, which made him wonder what else she was passionate about.

"You never told me how you ended up becoming the foreman here?"

She gave him a sideways glance. "That's because you never asked." She turned away from him and he trailed after her.

"So I'm asking now."

She stopped and stared up at the sky, her hands shoved into her pockets. "It was all I ever wanted to do. I started off as the foreman after I got back from college. Over time I took over more and more responsibilities, especially when Dad grew ill." She gave him a wry smile. "I guess I should have paid more attention to the books sooner, but Dad never let on that there was a problem, and I preferred being out here running things than stuck in an office."

Her eyes clouded over with a measure of pain and regret, before she masked her emotions. "So, what about you? How'd you end up running a multi-gazillion dollar ranching operation with your three brothers?"

He raised a brow. "A gazillion dollars?"

She grinned. "Close enough."

He shook his head, a small grin on his face. Where did she come up with this stuff? "When our father died, my older brother, Jacob, took over in his place. I guess it was just expected that after we were done with school, we would come back and help him. We all knew he couldn't do it alone."

"And that was a good thing—that you all came back to help him. Look at what the four of you have managed to accomplish together."

He shrugged. "I never really stopped to think of it like that. But I guess it is pretty cool when you do think about it. We've managed to pool our strengths into a successful business that we all love. It's hard work and long hours, but we really love what we do and that we get to do it together."

"Four workaholic bachelor brothers." A teasing glint lit up her eyes. "You think any of you will stop long enough to enjoy it, settle down and count your bazillion dollars?"

He stilled, the blood freezing in his veins. She was only joking, but her teasing words dredged up a host of unresolved feelings he'd been trying to forget.

"One of us has settled down," he said tightly, purposely avoiding her searching gaze.

She wanted to say more, *ask* more, it was right there on the tip of her tongue, but the sound of hoof beats in the distance drew her attention—thankfully—away from him.

A lone rider galloped towards them and as he drew closer, Jackson recognised him—it was the stable hand, Riley.

"What is it, Riley?" BJ asked, taking in the anxious look on his face.

"It's La Reina," he said breathlessly. "She's about to deliver her foal."

* * * *

La Reina was just that. She was the queen of Cottonmouth, their most prized mare, and she was delivering her very first foal.

BJ and Jackson raced back towards the stables, their mounts easily leaving poor Riley and his gelding in the wake of their dust—literally.

Five hours later, BJ stood just outside the stall nervously pacing back and forth.

"You should get some rest. If she has trouble, I can have someone come get you."

BJ stopped to stare up at Jackson. His beard shadowed his face. He was both rugged and sexy, as untamed and wild as the land just beyond the stables.

"No. I want to stay. I stay for all the mares, just in case." She was referring to the foaling process. Most of the time it went smoothly, and the mare delivered without any assistance, but there were a couple of instances where she'd needed to intervene.

"Is there anything I can get you then?"

"No. Why don't you go get some rest, yourself?"

He winked at her. "And miss out on this? Not a chance."

His statement made her think this was his first time witnessing a foaling, but three hours later, when they realised La Reina's foal was in breech position, she discovered he'd done this before, probably more times than she had.

By the time she returned from making a call to the veterinarian, Jackson had delivered La Reina's foal—much to her relief, and annoyance.

"Why didn't you tell me you'd done this before?" It was the first thing she said as soon as they entered the house after leaving the stable where La Reina and her new colt were resting.

"What? And let you think I wasn't the ignorant city boy you made me out to be? What would be the fun in that?"

She shot him a dark look. "You're so immature."

"You're just jealous that I delivered your mare's colt and not you." She didn't bother denying his words because he was right.

"I'm gonna grab a shower and change." He took off up the stairs, and BJ decided to do the same.

Fifteen minutes later she was back in the kitchen scrounging around in the cupboards for something to eat. She had assumed Jackson would head to bed, so she nearly jumped out of her skin when he crept up behind her.

"Shit. You scared me to death. I thought you were going to bed."

He frowned at her. "Bed? I haven't eaten in twelve hours. I'm starving." He looked over her shoulder into the pantry. "What were you thinking of making?"

"That's what I was trying to figure out when you nearly scared me half to death."

He grinned, drawing her attention to the tiny dimple in his cheek. That's when she realised he'd shaven. He was unquestionably handsome, although she found she had to squelch a twinge of disappointment that the rugged and untamed Jackson was now gone.

"Let's see what you have in here," he said reaching around her to grab for an item off the shelf. She let out a tiny gasp when his arm brushed against her right breast, her nipple instantly responding to the gentle caress.

They both stiffened, their gazes clashing. He was the first to recover, clearing his throat.

"Give me a second and I'll whip up some sandwiches." This time he was careful to avoid touching her when he reached into the pantry again.

The room was draped in tension, the awkwardness from their earlier moment still lingering around them. She sat down at the counter and watched him in silence while he threw together a late night dinner.

Finally, when she couldn't take the silence any longer she spoke. "So, you can cook, deliver foals *and* you're a millionaire? What can't you do Jackson Downing?"

He glanced up as he handed her a plate with a BLT on it. "Didn't you know? There's nothing I can't do. I'm damn near perfect."

She shook her head, hiding the grin behind her sandwich.

Perfect? *No.* But he was certainly not what she'd expected. From day one she'd misjudged him. She was just glad she hadn't let her earlier judgement of him keep her from seeing the real Jackson. They ate in silence until he noticed the slight grin on her face.

"What are you smiling about?"

She finished her sandwich and slid out of her chair to dump her empty plate into the sink. "Nothing really. Just thinking about how I didn't give you a chance when you first got here."

She turned but drew up short when she nearly collided with the solid wall of his chest.

"And that's funny?"

She shook her head. No it wasn't funny, but she couldn't say that out loud because she couldn't seem to find her voice when he was so close.

She wasn't sure what had happened exactly. One minute he'd been sitting across the counter and now he was standing there before her. His nearness sucked the air right out of her until she was foggy and lightheaded.

"Well, since we're being honest." He ran his thumb along the seam of her lips, and her heart thudded harder in her chest. "I guess I should tell you that I didn't give you a fair shot either."

That wasn't surprising. Most people didn't, but if her recollection of their initial meeting was correct, it was she who'd been difficult—not him. He'd tried being nice.

"I don't remember that." Her voice cracked. "I remember you being professional and polite—"

He silenced her with a single finger against her lips and moved closer until only inches separated them.

"When I met you I thought you were brash and abrasive—" Well, she was, wasn't she? "—nothing but a rude tomboy." She gasped when he pressed his lower body against her, the outline of his hard cock digging into her belly.

"And, I'm not all of those things?" She managed to stammer out.

"You are." He dipped his head to the curve of her neck and she shuddered against him. "But earlier today when you talked about Cottonmouth, there was a quiet passion in your eyes. And tonight as you handled La Reina's foal, you were full of tenderness." He pulled her closer. "There's a softness that you like to hide Bria, but it's there—deep down—it's there."

"Bria? My mother was the only person who called me that, and now you."

He lifted his head to stare into her eyes. He looked at her as if he could see straight to her soul, and an emotion she hadn't felt in a long time welled up inside her at the expression on his face. He made her feel vulnerable—in a good way—but still she was open and exposed to him, something she hadn't been with a man in some time.

"I like Bria. It's a beautiful name, and for me, it suits you better." He crooked his lips into a grin. "A beautiful name for a beautiful woman."

She averted her gaze to the floor. Every time he told her she was pretty, she felt like such a fraud. She pushed at his chest.

"Why are you doing this, Jackson?"

He looked at her as if she was dumb, as if to say, *the reason should be obvious.*

"I want you Bria. I have from the moment you cursed me out on your front porch." And just in case she had any doubt about that, he jerked his hips, pressing his cock deeper into her belly.

"I promised myself I wouldn't touch you." His voice was raspy and hoarse, and she stilled at the look in his eyes. Smouldering embers of heat leapt in his turquoise gaze, along with a storm of conflicting emotions.

"I said I would leave you alone."

After they'd nearly made love in that very same kitchen, she said she would leave him alone too. But it was hard to remember that vow with the heat of his body pressed against hers, while every inch of her burned for him.

"Don't." She wound her arms around his neck. "Don't leave me alone," she murmured as she lifted on her tip toes. This was a mistake—she knew it—but she couldn't stop herself and when Jackson dipped his head, and she met him mid-air to press her lips to his.

An explosion of pleasure and need erupted inside of her and she moaned into his mouth. He swept his tongue between her parted lips, tasting her, drinking from her and she shuddered against him.

Their bodies clashed together, their hands and lips going everywhere, searching beneath their clothing. Jackson arched into her, pressing her deeper into the sink's edge.

She didn't realise she'd winced until Jackson gathered her into his arms and laid her atop the kitchen table, sending place mats and the pepper shaker tumbling to the ground.

"Better?"

His dimpled grin was infectious and she found herself smiling back. "Much."

This time when their lips met, the kiss was gentle, slower, as they both took their time exploring each other. BJ twisted her hands in his hair, holding Jackson close, her legs encircling his hips to pull him deeper into her embrace.

His thick, hard erection was hot and heavy against her sex and she rocked against him, silently begging him to release himself from the confines of his pants and slide inside her. She'd never felt this way before—so wanton, so out of control. But with Jackson, he made her feel sexy, desirable, beautiful.

His hands slid along her legs until they reached the waistband of her pyjama bottoms. With steady hands, he undid the flimsy drawstring and pushed them over her hips, down her legs, until he had her out of them.

He stared at her with a sharp intensity that made her breath quicken in her chest, and molten heat swirl in her belly.

"You have gorgeous legs," he whispered reverently. "Long, toned, soft. They're perfect." They weren't. They were too skinny, but the way he looked at her made her think otherwise, and when his hands roamed over the bare skin of her legs, leaving tiny goose-bumps in their wake—she couldn't think, period.

He leant into her, seizing her lips, his hands curving beneath her to grab her ass. His tongue plundered her mouth, sending tingling flames of heat licking across her skin, as he gently massaged the firm globes of her ass.

She clung to him, her hands wandering over his broad shoulders, his chiselled back, before inching their way to his taut ass, where she returned the favour. Their kiss grew more urgent as he probed inside her mouth, demanding her complete surrender—and she gave it.

She arched deeper into him, her small breasts flattening against the muscled planes of his chest. She whimpered softly when he tore his lips from hers, until he dipped his head to the curve of her neck to stroke his tongue along the sensitive skin.

Jackson nibbled on her neck, his hands slipping between her legs. He slid one finger into her juicy cunt, the wet heat of her pussy surrounding him.

His deep groan mingled with her sharp cry of pleasure, her entire body shivering with need.

"Jackson." She whispered his name, unable to keep the plea from her voice. She wanted him inside her, the hard length of his cock battering against her tight walls. He knew what she wanted, what she needed, but he denied her and instead slipped another finger inside her.

It wasn't what she wanted, but it was more than enough. She rocked against his hand, meeting the deep stabbing strokes of his fingers, as her pussy filled with more juice. He stretched her, filled her, the pounding rhythm of his fingers brushing against her g-spot.

Her entire body vibrated around him, the tight buds of her nipples straining against her shirt. Jackson taunted and teased her, bringing her to the brink of climax before backing off again.

When he did it again, she pulled back from him, her eyes flashing with frustration.

"Just enjoy the tease," he said with a wicked grin. She wanted to tell him that it was easy for him to say since he wasn't the one on the verge of orgasm, but she never got the chance when he pressed his thumb against her clit, and massaged the tiny nub with just the right pressure.

She cried out his name, her back arching like a bow.

"That's it, Bria. Just let go."

She moaned louder. She was so close and when he slid down the length of her body and settled his head between her thighs, she knew she wouldn't last much longer.

He stroked his tongue through her wet slit before latching his lips around her clit and sucking hard.

"Jackson," she screamed his name, the onslaught of pleasure was so intense. Tunnelling her hands through his hair, she leant back, her thighs clamping around his head as he devoured her pussy.

His mouth consumed her, his hot tongue probing in and out of her tight hole. When he slipped two fingers inside her, the sensory overload was too much. She let out a long, low moan, her hips jerking off the table to meet his questing tongue and thrusting digits. She shuddered against him just before she erupted, the muscles of her pussy spasming from the force of her climax.

"Mmmm," he groaned against her cunt, lapping up her juices as tiny shocks of pleasure vibrated throughout her entire body.

When she finally quieted, he slid up her body and kissed her slowly and gently, leaving the taste of her juices in her mouth.

"You taste so good. I only wish I could have seen your face when you came."

She stroked her hand along his cheek. "You still can," she said with an impish smile, feeling emboldened.

He grinned down at her, but before he even said a word, she knew she wasn't going to get her ultimate wish for the night. She knew he wasn't going to make love to her.

"I wish I could." Regret filled his eyes. "But, I can't." He lifted himself off of her and helped put her pyjama bottoms back on. When she stood to her feet, she pretended to ignore the sticky wetness still lingering there.

Jackson was silent. She desperately wanted to ask what was stopping him from making love to her, what held him back, but she refused to push him. If he had his secrets, then he was free to keep them, so she was surprised when he clasped her face between his hands and said, "I want you Bria, there's no denying that."

He gave her a wry smile and gently nudged her belly with his still erect cock. Right. There was no doubt there. "But I came to Cottonmouth to get out of a sticky situation and get over a woman." He dropped his hands and stepped away from her.

"It's not fair to drag you into something when I don't know where my head or heart is right now. You deserve better."

He leant down to kiss her, the gentle kiss once again stoking the fire inside her, but before it could rage out of control, he lifted his head.

"Good night, Bria," he said, disappearing up the stairs.

She stared after him for a long while, thinking that whoever this woman was—the woman who still had Jackson's heart—was a very, very lucky woman.

A tiny pang shot through her heart as she allowed herself a foolish thought—what would it be like to be loved by Jackson Downing? To be the woman who claimed his heart?

Chapter Four

Jackson had just been preparing to sit down and go over the geologist's report on Cottonmouth's oil prospects when the doorbell rang.

Making his way towards the front door, he glanced at his watch. It was almost six o'clock in the evening. Who could have business at this time of night?

He opened the door and was momentarily taken aback. A statuesque redhead with curves for days and attitude to match stood on the doorstep with one hand planted on her rounded hips, and some sort of dress bag in the other.

"Hey handsome. Is BJ around?" She drawled out in a soft Southern accent, her eyes taking a leisurely trip along his frame. Any other day and any other time, he would have taken this woman's interest and ran with it, but that was before he'd met a golden-eyed spitfire who haunted his nightly dreams and claimed his waking thoughts.

"Last time I checked she was still out—" He turned towards the kitchen at the sound of a door slamming shut. "She's home," he finished with a small grin, just as BJ entered the living room.

The stacked redhead pushed past him. "You've been ignoring my calls."

BJ frowned at the dress bag in the redhead's hand. "Apparently for good reason. I told you I wasn't going."

Jackson raised an eyebrow. Going? Going where? He closed the front door, but instead of heading back to the den he stood off to the side.

"You're going, BJ. You promised me—"

"I don't have a date or a dress."

"Dress taken care of," the woman said, holding up the bag. She glanced over her shoulder at Jackson. "And what about him? He could be your date."

Jackson looked at BJ. "Date for what?"

"Nothing."

The woman with the dress bag glared at BJ, before turning to him to extend her hand. "I'm sorry. I didn't introduce myself. My name is Teresa Mae West, BJ's oldest and dearest friend—" She rolled her eyes when BJ snorted. "Twice a year I host a charity fundraiser, which BJ always donates to, but never attends."

Jackson shook her hand. "Jackson Downing. Nice to meet you, Teresa Mae West. Interesting name."

She gave him a wry smile. "Parents thought it was funny."

Funny. No doubt. But from what he could tell, it definitely suited her.

"So, this fundraiser—I'm guessing it's black tie and you want me to take Bria."

Teresa raised her eyebrows, shooting BJ a quizzical look from over his shoulder.

"That's what he calls me and just so you know, no matter what he says, I'm still not going."

Jackson turned to BJ. "At least try on the dresses. She did come all this way to bring them to you."

"She only lives two miles away." BJ narrowed her eyes. "And why waste everyone's time and try on dresses I'm not going to wear?"

"You promised me you would go this time. And you *never* break a promise," Teresa said.

BJ was trapped and she knew it. And in that moment, she wanted to be anywhere else but there. Seconds ticked by while BJ and Teresa stared each other down. Finally, BJ relented with a long suffering sigh. "Fine." She folded her arms across her chest. "I'll go, but after this—I swear I'm severing our friendship."

"You say that at least five times a year." Teresa shoved the dress bag at BJ and had Jackson not caught it, it would have landed on the floor. Jackson gave her a look to let her know he thought she was being childish. The one she shot back told him she wanted him to stay out of it. He grinned. Not a chance.

"So am I invited too?" He asked Teresa.

"No."

"Of course, BJ needs a date," Teresa said, pointedly ignoring BJ's outburst.

She twisted on her heels then, and walked towards the door. "I need to head home now. Nice meeting you, Jackson. Looking forward to seeing you *both* next Friday."

BJ mumbled something under her breath that sounded an awful lot like *you're both going to hell for this,* but Jackson couldn't be sure.

When the door closed behind Teresa, he turned to BJ.

"She seems like a nice woman. You should feel good that you're doing something for charity. I'm sure we'll have fun."

Her eyes darkened to whisky brown pools. "Nice? Teresa's not nice. And let's be honest, you don't give a damn about that charity dinner or how much fun we could have. The only reason why you even agreed to go was because you think she's hot."

He lifted a brow. Teresa *was* hot, but she wasn't the one he wanted to see in a dress on Friday night.

"Teresa's hot? You know what, I really hadn't noticed."

She spun away from him and stomped towards the kitchen. "Liar."

"It'll be fun, and you know it," he called after her, as she disappeared into the kitchen. He smiled when she didn't respond. BJ always had a comeback, so the fact that she was speechless told him she was too mad to bother forming words.

Somewhere deep down, he felt just a bit sorry for her—but only a bit. He took the dress bag upstairs and laid it across her bed. He itched to peek inside, but he didn't want to spoil it. He would wait until he saw her on Friday—it would be that much sweeter. BJ dressed up and on his arm—he couldn't wait.

* * * *

BJ glanced at herself in the mirror, a frown on her face. She could not believe she'd actually been forced into doing something so heinous, so despicable, something that was completely beneath her. She could not believe she was wearing a *dress*. She never wore dresses. She absolutely hated them.

This was all Teresa's fault, but she couldn't forget Jackson's role in this too. She would have probably been able to brush her friend off, yet again, had it not been for Jackson's meddling.

"Damn it." She sucked her finger where the zipper pinched her skin. Yet another reason why she hated dresses, skirts, gowns—anything of that ilk. They were right up there with high heels. BJ gave her feet—which at the moment were encased in four-inch bone hued sandals—a disparaging look. She'd be lucky if she made it out of the house without tripping and breaking her neck.

"Are you ready?" Jackson called out from the other side of the door.

She groaned. *No.*

She didn't want to give Jackson the satisfaction of knowing she was so inept at this dress up thing, but there was no getting around it. She'd been trying for the last five minutes and it was clear that her zipper was stuck.

"I can't get my zipper up."

There was a pregnant pause on the other side, before Jackson said slowly, "Are you asking for help?"

She gritted her teeth. What did he think?

"Yes," she bit out.

Not more than a second ticked by before the door swung open.

"You don't have to look so smug about this," she said at the smirk on Jackson's face.

Smug? Not even close. It just happened to be the most benign expression he could seem to muster up the moment he got his first glimpse of her.

He let out a low whistle. There was no doubt BJ was a natural beauty. In faded shirts and jeans, she exuded a provocative sensuality that was impossible to ignore. But tonight, she was simply stunning.

Her hair framed her lovely face, the wiry curls straightened into a sleek style that fell to the middle of her back. The soft cream of the dress hugged her gentle curves, dipping just low enough to reveal the swells of her breasts, and falling at her knees, giving him a tantalising view of her smooth legs that seemed to go on for days.

"Wow. I'm almost speechless."

"*Almost* speechless, but still *not* speechless."

Her lovely topaz eyes flashed with fire, but hidden in their depths was a small ember of relief. She'd been afraid he wouldn't like what he saw. He swept his gaze over the bronzed beauty. Not a chance.

"Turn around," he said.

She gave him a puzzled look.

"You said you needed help with your zipper."

"Oh, right." She nodded and turned her back to him, treating him to the sight of the cutest most unexpected tattoo along the smooth skin of her back.

"An angel?" He said when he stood behind her.

"A wha—oh. My tattoo. I always forget about that."

He stared at the image of a beautiful angel, with her black wings stretched out across BJ's upper back.

"It's lovely. When did you get it?"

She stiffened, and he wondered if she would answer him, when she said in a small voice. "I had it done on the one-year anniversary of my mother's death. The face of the angel was drawn from an old photo of her."

He glanced down again. He could see the resemblance now. "She was beautiful."

He heard the smile in her voice. "She was."

Jackson zipped her up, and when he was done he settled his hands against her shoulders—he couldn't stand not touching her any longer.

"You look absolutely amazing tonight." He spun her around. "But you're beautiful in whatever you wear—jeans, a dress, a sack." He smiled.

She tucked a strand of hair behind her ear, her fingers trembling slightly. "Thanks. That's nice of you to say."

He frowned at her. "I wasn't saying it to be nice. I said it because it's the truth." And it was. Dress or jeans, she was beautiful. Although, truth be told, her best look would be in nothing at all.

Despite what he said, he could still see the denial in her eyes, and when she opened her mouth to protest he let out a short sigh of frustration.

"Just say thank you, Bria. Acknowledge that I find you beautiful, and simply accept the compliment." Her eyes widened at the edge in his voice, but she nodded, her voice small as she said, "Thank you."

He relaxed, pleased that for once she didn't fight him. This time, however, he refused to let the issue drop. Ever since he'd discovered she had issues about her looks, he'd been waiting for a moment like this to broach the subject.

"Why is it so hard for you to accept that I think you're beautiful?"

She stiffened, her eyes dipping to the floor, but he dragged her gaze back to him with a finger under her chin. "Talk to me Bria."

She let out a jagged breath, and he wondered if she would refuse to answer him, when she finally said in a small voice, "It was never something that anyone said. I just saw how people, men especially, reacted to my mother and Natalie when they met them and then there was how they reacted to me."

She shrugged, her eyes taking on a faraway look. "I just always felt like the ugly duckling around them, and I guess over time I came to believe I was just that—ugly and awkward."

He cupped her cheek, finally understanding, and his heart ached for the beautiful young girl she'd once been whose only flaw was that she'd been different. "I know you will probably think this is corny, but there is no set standard when it comes to beauty. Believe me when I tell you that I think you're beautiful inside and out."

He pulled her closer, his gaze boring into her. He wanted her to see the truth in his eyes so there would never be any doubts in her mind. "I thought you were beautiful from the moment I met you. Now, believe me when I say you drove me crazy, but I loved how you stood up to me." He touched her hair, "And I think it's beautiful how your curls catch the sun in the morning." He stroked her cheek. "And how your skin glows at dusk." He stroked his fingers across her entire face. "I love that your eyes turn gold when you're emotional, but most of all I love your sass and boldness, how you're passionate about everyone and everything around you."

His heart clenched at the awe in her eyes. She deserved a man who would love her, cherish her, make her feel secure when she doubted herself. He ignored the lump in his throat at the thought that he could be that man, that he *wanted* to be that man—if only his life weren't so full of complications, weren't haunted by ghosts from the past.

He leant down to kiss her full lips, plump and glossy from her lipstick. It was supposed to be a quick peck, but the instant their lips touched he went up in flames. Heat surged through his blood, his cock growing hard as a rock in seconds. His hands dipped to her ass, pulling her close as he claimed her with his mouth.

He had no idea how long they would have stood there locked in each other's arms or how far their kiss would have gone, but when his watch beeped at the top of the hour it snapped them both back to the present.

"We better go," he said, reluctantly easing himself out of her arms. "It's already seven o'clock."

"Right. Wouldn't want to be late." The false chirpiness of her voice made him smile.

"Well, just remember, you're doing this for charity." He grinned down at her, ushering her from the room with his hand against her back, pointedly ignoring the dark glower on her face.

"I'm not doing this for charity because I've already donated to Teresa's cause. I'm doing this because you and my best friend conspired against me."

"It'll be fun tonight, trust me."

The expression on her face told him she didn't trust him on this at all, but she kept her thoughts to herself, as she followed him out the door.

* * * *

"So that hunk of a man managed to get you into a dress after all? I never would have believed it had I not seen it with my own eyes."

BJ glared at Teresa. "You two practically blackmailed me. It wasn't like I had much of a choice."

"Oh, you had a choice." Her green eyes twinkled. "So, are you just going to tell me what's going on with you and Jackson Downing or am I gonna have to pry it out of you?"

BJ took a sip from the glass of wine in her hand, trying to delay the inevitable. "There's really nothing going on."

"Nothing?" She glanced between BJ and Jackson, who stood a few feet away chatting with other guests, although his gaze kept straying back to BJ every few seconds. "Doesn't look like nothing. He can hardly keep his eyes off you."

"That's because for once I'm not covered in horse shit. He's probably still in shock."

"Probably. But I know there's more to it than that." Teresa pinned BJ with her green gaze, until BJ let out a long sigh and finally relented.

"You're so nosy, you know that? We just kissed and fooled around a bit, but that's it. *That's it*," she added at the speculative look on Teresa's face.

"So are you two dating?"

"I wouldn't go that far."

"But you like him."

BJ cast a quick glance over at Jackson. She smiled. "I do."

"Oh, we're going to talk." Teresa wagged her finger in BJ's face. "I have to make my rounds, but you better believe we are going to talk about how you've been keeping secrets from your best friend—"

"I haven't been keeping secrets, just been swamped with work."

Teresa snorted. "I don't believe you. But when we catch up, we will talk all about that, and the ridiculous look you have on your face."

"What ridiculous look?"

Teresa's eyes danced with mischief. "Oh, that goofy dreamy expression you get whenever you look at Jackson."

She did not look goofy. Did she? She opened her mouth to argue but Teresa was already breezing away, floating off into the crowd where she would spend the rest of the evening mingling.

She did *not* look goofy *or* dreamy whenever she looked at Jackson. She took another sip of wine. That was just Teresa trying to goad her.

Jackson still stood off in the corner talking to a few people. As BJ made her way over to them, a hand grasped her arm and spun her around.

She paused for a beat until she recognised who it was. "Lou. Hi."

"Hey, BJ." His eyes roamed over her. "Wow, you look amazing."

"Thanks."

She was just about to tell him that most girls' eyes didn't fall at chest level, when his gaze finally snapped to her face.

"What are you doing here?" she asked, since she now had his full attention.

He lifted his hand and that's when she finally saw the tray of hors d'oeuvres. "Side job," he said with a grin. "What about you? I never thought this would be your kind of scene."

She wanted to say neither had she. "My best friend is the host. I was kind of coerced into coming."

"Well, I'm glad you did come." He leant into her. "You really do look lovely. Maybe one day you'll finally let me take you out to dinner—"

"I wouldn't hold my breath if I were you."

Lou straightened to his full height. His expression was tight as he met Jackson's stony gaze.

She placed her hand against Jackson's chest, but he wouldn't budge. Instead of moving backward, he actually inched closer to the young man. "It was nice seeing you again, Lou. Have a good night."

She was relieved when Lou tipped his head in a nod and moved on, since it was apparent that Jackson had no intention of going anywhere.

She rounded on him. "I really wish you would lighten up with Lou. He's—"

"Dance with me." He didn't wait for her response, and instead seized her arm and hauled her towards the dance floor. She glared at him when he pulled her into his arms, but didn't resist, mostly because she didn't want to make a scene.

"I want you to quit it with the warden act. Lou's a good kid. He means no harm."

Jackson leant back to peer down at her, and she noticed a small vein throbbed over one eyebrow. "He means no harm? Is that why I caught him with his eyes glued to your chest? Lou is not a kid. You would do well to realise that."

Fury shook her. She wasn't a child to be dictated to. "Alright. So he's an adult. So what? He's barely legal. I like Lou as a friend, but I'm not interested in him like that."

"But it's obvious he's interested in you or he wouldn't have invited you out to dinner."

"Is having dinner a crime now?"

His expression darkened. "With a man who wants to be more than your friend? Yes, it is."

She couldn't believe they were having this discussion. He was acting like a jealous Neanderthal for no reason. "You're being ridiculous. I had friends long before you barrelled into my life, and I have no intention of ending those friendships just because you're irrational. You have no say in who I keep company with—"

"You're wrong, Bria." His arms tightened around her, his eyes swirling with dark clouds. "When I'm eating a woman's pussy out every night, *all* night, then I think I get to have a say in who she's seeing, who she's fucking."

Her cheeks grew hot at the image of him between her legs, his mouth pressed against her sex. Although they had yet to take that final step, the past week had been filled with him in her bed as they pleasured each other in every way imaginable. But, no self-respecting gentleman would have brought that up at a time like this, especially with people all around who were now staring at them.

She stopped in the middle of the dance floor. So much for not making a scene.

"We're done here." She twisted on her heels and stomped out of there before she let loose the curses she had for him on the tip of her tongue.

She made her way outside, the cool night air whipping across her face. Teresa's ranch was probably the most impressive in all of Hockley. It was one of the few with a formal ballroom, which was where Teresa held her charity events and fundraisers. BJ couldn't get away from there fast enough. She marched down the stairs, her heeled feet digging into the hard, unyielding earth.

She knew this land almost as well as she knew her own, so on instinct she found herself heading towards the stables. She was halfway there when a hand closed around her arm. She let out a tiny yelp, before she was spun around. Anger narrowed her eyes when she saw who it was.

"Damn it, you walk fast. Especially for someone who claims she never wears heels."

She wrenched her arm from his grasp, and settled her hands against her hips. "What can I say? I guess it's my long skinny legs."

She hadn't sought to draw his attention to her legs on purpose, but her comment did just that, as his gaze took a leisurely trip along the length of her legs.

"Skinny, no.   Now long?" His brow arched. "Endlessly."

Her breath caught in her chest at the desire that leapt in his gaze as he inched closer.

"I'm a jealous prick. I know it. I just have this thing about not sharing what's mine."

She tipped her head to the side. "Yours?" That was news to her.

"Mine." Her heart skipped a beat, the intensity of his gaze threatening to set her on fire.

"I'm not interested in Lou." Or any other man for that matter, but she had trouble forming words when his thumb brushed across her lower lip.

"Good." Was all he said, his head dipping to crush his lips to hers.

She yielded under the forceful demand of his mouth, her tongue shooting out to tangle with his. He kissed her thoroughly, the weight of his mouth possessive. She arched into him, her arms twisting behind his neck, her breasts flattening against the solid muscles of his hard chest.

She whimpered when he pulled away from her, but he silenced her with a single finger against her lips.

"We gotta get out of the open field, but I'm not going to make it back to the ranch. Hell, I doubt I will be able to last long enough to make it to the car."

She flashed him a mischievous grin as she grabbed his hand and led the way. She had the perfect place.

"Where are you taking me?"

"Just trust me."

Seconds later they stood on the other side of a large open air structure.

His forehead wrinkled. "A barn?"

She pushed open the doors. "It doesn't have a roof, just rafters." She tugged him by the hand into the barn, and shut the door. "We can see the stars from inside."

He followed her gaze towards the sky, before turning to her with a small smile.

"I've never made love under the stars," he whispered, enfolding her into his arms.

Her eyes softened as she rested against his chest. "Well then, I'm glad I'm your first."

Chapter Five

Jackson lowered his head to capture her lips again. He took his time tasting her, exploring every inch of her mouth with his searching tongue. It was a struggle to take it slow, but he wanted to savour every second.

Her hands plunged into his hair, holding him closer. She kissed him back with a passionate urgency that made his blood simmer with heat. He paused, drawing in a ragged breath, before lightly kissing a trail along her collarbone.

"Jackson." His name on her lips was the sweetest thing he'd ever heard.

He lifted his head. "You're absolutely breathtaking tonight." An ember of doubt flashed in her eyes, but this time she accepted the compliment. He wanted to reassure her that she was not only breathtaking but beautiful, and amazing as well, but decided to show her with actions instead of words.

He shrugged out of his tuxedo jacket and dress shirt, spreading them over the scattered hay before gently laying her on the ground. Covering her with his body, he cupped her face in his hands, and simply stared into her eyes that were now the colour of silver under the gleam of the moonlight.

His next breath caught in his chest as he held her gaze, the quiet vulnerability he glimpsed in her eyes causing a lump to form in his throat. She was remarkable to him in every way. She was tough as nails, smart as a whip and full of sass, and yet there was a gentleness to her that called to his soul and raised his instincts to cherish and protect her.

He froze when he realised what was happening—he was falling for her. It was inconceivable. Months ago he'd been battling his feelings for Camille, but he now recognised those feelings for what they were—a combination of lust and a deep, abiding friendship. They were a pale comparison to what he felt for BJ.

She touched his face. "What is it?"

He wanted to tell her, but he wasn't ready. He needed to sort a lot of things out within himself, but also with Camille and Jacob, before he revealed his feelings.

"Nothing." He cupped her cheek. "Are you uncomfortable?"

She smiled as she shook her head, her hand curling in his hair to pull him in for another kiss. All thoughts of Camille, Jacob and the past vanished the moment their lips touched.

He skimmed his hands down the length of her body, sucking in a sharp breath when he reached the bare skin of her thighs. He hiked the skirt of her dress up to her hips, his hands dipping between her legs to remove her panties. He moved down the length of her body and settled between her parted thighs, his eyes dancing with mischief just before he lowered his head to drink from her pussy.

"Jackson." She cried out, her back arching off the makeshift bed.

He closed his eyes, the sweet musk of her arousal filling his lungs. She was wet and juicy, the taste of her like honey on his tongue. He devoured her with his mouth, sucking on the hardened nub, flicking it with his tongue until she was writhing and panting before him. Hot juices flowed from her cunt and he lapped them up as he speared her with his fingers, dragging a long, harsh moan from her lips. Her body began to tremble and vibrate all around him, her thighs trapping his head between her legs. Her moans grew louder, as her fingers dug deeper into his scalp. He knew the moment she came, her entire body stiffened as tangy, sweet wetness gushed from her pussy to fill his mouth.

"Jacksonnnnn." She screamed out as her body shook from the tremulous force of her orgasm.

While spasms still racked her, he released his cock and covered her body, surging into her clenching heat. She screamed louder and he squeezed his eyes shut, forcing air into his lungs to keep himself from splintering apart right then and there. The tight, wet vise of her pussy gripped him as he began to move in and out of her, and he knew he wouldn't be able to last for long.

She felt too good around him, surrounding him, drawing him deeper and deeper into her body until he wasn't sure who was claiming who or who was taking whom?

Those longs legs he'd fantasised about since the day he'd met her, extended up to his shoulders and clasped at the ankle behind his back.

"Bria," he rasped, the new position sending him deeper. He pinned her hips, trying to still her movements. He would never last if she kept meeting him thrust for thrust.

It didn't work. He felt his balls draw up tight to his body, just as a tingle shot up from the base of his spine.

"Bria. Oh God." He surged into her once, twice, three more times before he shattered. He swore he blacked out as he came, filling her up with his hot cum.

He collapsed atop her, his entire body jerking as he continued to ejaculate inside her. He closed his eyes, as he struggled to even his breathing. She stroked his sweat slick back, her long limbs sliding up and down his legs.

When he could finally draw in a full breath of air, he rolled off of her.

For a long time they laid there in silence, staring up at the twinkling stars.

He turned to glance at her when her breathing grew low and even. She was asleep.

He let out a long yawn, his lids growing heavy. It was the perfect night and with the perfect woman. He couldn't have imagined a more perfect moment for their first time together. He looked up at the heavens again, a smile on his face. Moments later he drifted off to sleep with BJ nestled in his arms.

* * * *

"What are you two doing here?"

"Do you answer your front door in nothing but a towel nowadays? Where are your clothes, bro?" Jason said as he pushed past Jackson, with Jeff at his heels. Jackson glowered at his two younger brothers, slamming the door behind them.

"I had to rush to get down here. You two were *leaning* on the bell."

"Yeah and what took you so lon—"

"Jackson?"

He let out an inward groan when BJ chose that moment to come down the stairs still wet from their shower, with nothing but a towel wrapped around her body. He fought the urge to strangle his brothers when he glimpsed the appreciative looks on their faces.

"It's nothing Bria. Just my younger brothers."

She stopped on the stairs, her gaze darting between the three of them. "Oh. Hi."

"I'll be back upstairs soon—"

"You know what, I'll just go change." She looked uncomfortable. "I'll only be a few minutes."

"Bria—" She was already headed back upstairs. "Damn it." He rounded on his brothers, who both wore shit eating grins. He wanted to pummel them.

"I'm going to ask one more time, what the hell are you two doing here?"

The look passed between them said it all.

Fury bubbled up inside of him. "Jacob," he said flatly.

"None of us had heard from you in awhile," Jeff offered by way of explanation.

"So what? Jacob sent you two instead because he didn't think I would pick up if he called."

Jason shrugged as if to say, *pretty much.*

"You are all ridiculous." He glared at them. He couldn't believe Jacob had sent them to check up on him. What? Did Jacob think he'd flung himself off a bridge or something absurd?

"I need to go change."

"Yeah. About that..." Jason looked towards the stairs. "So, new girlfriend?"

"Definitely a hottie," Jeff added

Jackson scowled at both of them. "Her name is Bria. She's Natalie's sister and the foreman here and we're trying to sort out what we are at the moment, which is why it would be a big help if you two left, like, *now*."

Jason raised a brow. "So you're over Camille?"

"And so soon?" Asked Jeff.

"None of that is any of your business."

"Does Bria know about Camille?" Jason chimed in.

Jackson closed his eyes and counted to ten. He didn't need this right now.

"No. She doesn't know," he bit out. "And I'm not planning to tell her anytime soon, and neither are you, if you wind up staying longer than the five minutes I want you to."

"Oh, we're staying." Jeff glanced towards the stairs again, and the expression on his face had Jackson seeing red.

"Don't even think about it. I'm not sharing her."

That raised some eyebrows. "Why not?" Jason questioned.

"Because I like her." *I think I love her* is what he wanted to add, but he wanted BJ to be the first person to hear those words, not his younger brothers.

"That's never stopped you before."

Jackson gave Jeff a long, hard look. "She's different." He stared Jason down to be sure the message was clear. "Stay away from her. *Both* of you."

Their mutual nods tempered his anger, but the smirks on their faces raised his ire all over again. Damn it. Why had they shown up at that very moment? He'd just broken through BJ's seemingly impenetrable wall the night before. Their lovemaking in the barn had been magical. He didn't want to run the risk of having her withdraw from him, and one slip from either of his brothers about Jacob and Camille would no doubt send her retreating from him as fast as she could.

"I need to change. Do me a favour and disappear while I'm gone."

* * * *

BJ traded her terry cloth towel for a pair of jeans and a work shirt and headed back downstairs, but stopped on the first step when she heard her name.

She hadn't planned to eavesdrop. She'd been all set to turn around, go back upstairs and wait for Jackson. But her curiosity got the best of her, especially when she heard one of Jackson's brothers ask if he was over Camille?

She stilled, her ears perking up. Neither Jackson, nor his brothers revealed much else about Camille and her relationship with Jackson, but she was able to fill in the missing pieces. He'd been involved with this woman—apparently not too long ago—and from what she could tell it must have been quite a break-up for his brothers to arrive unannounced to check up on him.

She gasped, the wave of jealousy that swamped her was so unexpected and so overpowering. Jackson had shared pieces of his story with her already. She knew he'd hesitated with her because his heart still belonged to another. Although she'd been aware of this before getting involved with him, it still didn't make it any easier to hear.

She started to turn around again, but stopped when she heard what Jackson said about *sharing* her. Sharing her?

Why the hell would they want to do that? The Downing brothers were notoriously good looking and known ladies' men. They didn't need to share women—women were the ones who had to share *them*.

Her heart did a little flutter at Jackson's declaration. He liked her? Thought she was different? She wasn't against being shared by the Downing men—after all, they *were* fine. But it warmed her to know Jackson was possessive about her, although from the way he'd handled Lou, she'd already gotten a pretty good glimpse of his jealous side.

A renewed sense of hope flared inside of her. She still stood a chance. Jackson may have loved—may *still* love this Camille woman—but his words made it clear that at some point he could learn to love her too.

She tiptoed back upstairs, clinging to that thought with a smile on her face.

* * * *

Jackson knew it was too much to ask for younger brothers who actually listen to him and do what they were told.

"Didn't I tell you two to get lost?" he said fifteen minutes later as he entered the kitchen.

Jeff's gaze was glued to BJ, a silly grin plastered across his face. "Yes, but the lovely Bria told us we could stay for as looooonnng as we wanted."

His gaze snapped to the woman in question, who gave him a sheepish grin.

"They drove all this way."

He didn't give a damn. They were going to fuck this up, he knew it.

"One night." He slumped into a chair. "Tomorrow morning you two ride out of here."

His attention went back to BJ when she moved towards the door. "I need to get going," she said and he instantly shot to his feet.

"It's Saturday. Take a day off."

Her smile was wistful. "Wish I could, but you stay and enjoy your time with your brothers."

He cast a baleful glance towards them. Not likely. He wanted to enjoy his time with her, preferably twisted in his bed sheets.

"Keep your phone on. I'll meet up with you in an hour and help you finish up early."

"You don—"

He silenced her with a kiss, pointedly ignoring the loud throat clearing behind him. His brothers soon disappeared from his consciousness completely as she melted into him, her mouth fusing with his.

He could have stayed locked in her arms forever, but he needed air. He lifted his head, a smile curling his lips at the dreamy expression on her face.

"I'll see you soon," he whispered.

She nodded, still dazed. "Nice meeting you both," she called to Jason and Jeff from over his shoulder. "I'll see you soon," she said to him in a low, breathless voice and then walked out the kitchen door.

He stared at her all too tempting backside until it disappeared from sight.

"Damn, you got it bad. Almost as bad as Jacob..."

"If not worse," chirped Jason.

He grimaced. Trust his brothers to snap him back to reality.

He turned around and flopped back down into his chair. He had twenty-four hours until his brothers got lost. These were probably going to be the longest twenty-four hours of his entire life.

Chapter Six

Wow. Whoa. There were *two* of them and they both looked like hunky Jacksons. She'd seen pictures of the Downing brothers in dozens of magazines, but now that she was face-to-face, she could safely say that the pictures didn't do them any justice. Teresa drew in a deep breath, fighting the urge to fan herself.

"Um, is BJ here?"

"No BJ here. But we are. Good evening." One of the handsome hunks stuck out his hand, a dangerously wicked smile curving his lips. "Jeff Downing."

She shook his hand, her eyes widening when a bolt of heat shot up her arm.

"Hi. I'm Jason. This idiot's brother." His eyes were softer, gentler and when she shook his hand, it was just that, a handshake. She focused on Jason. She felt safer with him than with his roguish brother.

"Do you know when BJ will be back?" She directed her question to Jason, but Jeff answered, forcing her to look at him.

"BJ? Who's BJ?"

What did he mean who was BJ? "The woman who lives here."

Their brows shot towards the sky and Jeff said, "The only woman I know who lives here is Bria."

Right. It was *Bria* now. "Same person. BJ stands for Bria Jaslene." She decided not to add, *and the only people who call her that are you and Jackson.*

"Do you know when she'll be home?"

"Oh, she's home now." Jeff thumbed towards the back. "She's out back getting it on with Jackson."

"Really?" Her lips quirked into a grin. If BJ was making out with hunky Jackson then it could be awhile. She glanced between Jason and Jeff. Jeff still scared her, not in a bad way, but in a *he's-big-trouble* way. But they were undoubtedly easy on the eyes. There could be worse ways to idle away her time.

"I'll wait for her."

She brushed between the two of them, biting back a gasp when Jeff closed the distance and leant towards her, a wolfish grin on his face.

"I was hoping you would say that."

* * * *

Making out quickly turned into making love.

"Jackson. Stop that." She swatted at his hand on her ass. "Your brothers might see us."

"They're all the way in the other room."

The noises coming from the other room told her that Jackson was right. She stopped at the sound of a throaty laugh. There was a woman with them. She listened for a beat.

"Teresa's here."

"And she's alone with my younger brothers? We may want to shout out a warning so they have enough time to put their clothes back on."

She frowned at Jackson from over her shoulder. "Are all of you Downings players?"

His answering grin was slow and sexy. "I'm a lover, not a player. But those two? Well, they're another story."

She rolled her eyes. "Whatever, Casanova," she said and marched into the living room, but came to an abrupt halt when she saw Teresa with Jason and Jeff.

"Teresa?"

She smiled at BJ from between Jeff's legs, her head upside down. "Hey, BJ." She snapped up, sending Jeff sprawling to the floor.

"What are you two doing?"

"It's Twister."

BJ gave her best friend a vexed look. "I know what it *is*. What the hell are you doing playing it in my living room?"

"Got bored waiting for you two to come inside." Teresa gave her chest a pointed look, right before she mouthed, *Fix your shirt.*

She glanced down, heat creeping into her cheeks when she noticed she'd missed a button.

She hurriedly closed her shirt. "So, what's up?" She asked, trying to ignore the embarrassment swamping over her. The knowing twinkle in Teresa's gaze made her cheeks grow hotter, but thankfully her friend let her off the hook, and pretended as if nothing had happened.

"I stopped by to find out what you were doing this weekend. Gotta take a road trip to Lehigh for business tomorrow. Wanted to see if you wanted to come."

BJ smiled. They were notorious for taking ill-fated and eventful road trips.

"Hey, that's just a half hour from Macon. Jackson, didn't you say you had to drive back for business on Tuesday? We should all drive together."

She glanced up at Jackson who looked like he wanted to kill Jeff.

"No, we shouldn't. I'm actually thinking you two should leave tonight, and let Teresa and BJ drive in peace."

BJ turned to face him. "But then you will have to drive by yourself. Doesn't make any sense if you have to be there next week too. We could all just go together."

Jackson nodded towards his brothers. "Trust me, you don't want to take a five-hour road trip with these clowns."

She wrinkled her brow. "Really, Jackson? How bad could it possibly be?"

* * * *

"I don't want to say I told you so."

Her eyes shot daggers at Jackson. "Shut it."

He looked like he had no intention of shutting anything as he leant back against his car with a smug grin on his face.

"Aren't you happy I convinced you and Teresa to take a separate car?"

She let out a long sigh. "We made it here. That's the main thing."

He chuckled. "Barely."

Barely was right. In the end Jackson had decided to drive alone and follow behind in his car, while his two brothers led the way.

"Let's see. They got us lost, even though they own a GPS. They ran out of gas. Got us kicked out of a restaurant. What else?"

Her lips thinned into a tight line. "I got it. Your brothers suck at road trips, you knew this and you tried to spare me. Happy?"

He straightened to his full height and pulled her into his arms. "Now, I am."

Her heart skipped a beat. When he said things like that, she forgot all about how aggravating he could be when he was right and how tired she was after the road trip from hell.

He lowered his mouth, and she met his lips in a searing kiss. He claimed her with hot, deep strokes of his tongue, making her melt against him. She entwined her limbs with his, as he enfolded her into his embrace. The hard, steel strength of him surrounded her, making her feel cherished and protected—something she'd never felt with a man until she'd met Jackson.

The porch door banged shut bringing an abrupt end to their blissful kiss. They sprang apart, but Jackson didn't let her go. He kept his arm draped around her waist, cuddling her close.

With her body pressed to his, she felt the instant a chill settled over him. His features became drawn, his jaw tight.

"Jacob? I thought you were out of town."

BJ immediately recognised the man towering over them from the porch as the eldest brother, Jacob Downing. He stared at her, his handsome face twisted into a scowl. Jackson must have felt her stiffen because his hand settled against the small of her back, his fingers drawing lazy circles against her skin.

"I decided to come back early. Wasn't expecting you for a couple more days."

Jackson glanced at her. "Bria's friend had business in Lehigh. Decided to drive up here with her."

"Bria? " Jacob's eyebrow lifted. "Natalie's little sister?"

"One in the same." She gave him a tentative smile. "You must be Jacob. It's nice to meet you."

"Likewise." He nodded politely, but she got the distinct impression that he was being just that—polite.

The air around them was thick with tension and her eyes darted between Jackson and Jacob. It was obvious from Jackson's rigid posture and Jacob's guarded gaze that something had transpired between them, something that left them both wary around one another.

The door opened again and a beautiful black woman breezed out, her violet dress moulding beautifully to her voluptuous curves. BJ felt like a gangly little girl, compared to the statuesque beauty.

"Jacob, honey—" The woman's almond shaped eyes fell on her before sliding to Jackson.

"Jackson. What a surprise. It's so good to see you." There was a deep regret in the woman's gaze when she looked at him that was completely at odds with her cheerful greeting.

The tension coursing through Jackson's body was so strong, BJ could feel it vibrating though her own.

"It's good to see you too, Camille." He nodded. "I would like to introduce you to Bria." He looked at her. "Bria, this is my brother's wife, Camille."

Blood rushed to her ears at the same time her throat closed up. Camille? *Camille*. It didn't even take her a second to put the pieces together. Camille was Jackson's former lover, the woman who still held his heart. She glanced between Jackson and Camille. She couldn't breathe.

Jackson's brow knitted with worry. "Bria, you okay?" He whispered.

No, she wasn't okay. She felt sick.

She backed away from him, and when Jackson reached for her, she shook her head.

"Your brother's wife? You're still in love with your brother's wife?" She rasped in a low voice, for his ears only.

The blood drained from his face. "How did you—"

"Find out? Does it really matter?"

"Just give me a chance to explain." His eyes pleaded with her.

Explain? She would have laughed in his face had they been alone. No matter what he said, it would never make any of this right.

"I'm going to get a hotel for the night." She turned towards the porch, trying her best to keep her fake, brittle smile plastered across her face. "It was nice meeting you both. Have a good night."

She didn't wait for a response. She walked away from the house as fast as her wobbly legs would carry her as she reached into her pocket for her cell phone.

Dialling the only person she knew who could help her right now, she fought back the emotions clogging her throat. Jackson had had an affair with his brother's wife. She couldn't believe she'd been so wrong about him, that she'd misjudged his character and fallen in love with a man who could betray his own brother.

The phone rang twice before a sleepy voice answered, "Hey, BJ."

"Hey. I know it's late, b—but can you come and get me?"

* * * *

Jackson watched helplessly as BJ stalked off. "Would you two excuse me?"

"Why don't you just give her a moment alone?"

Jackson glared at his brother. He knew Jacob well enough to know what he was thinking. Jacob thought BJ was a rebound, that he'd brought her back to Macon to prove to him and Camille that he was over Camille. Jacob was wrong.

Jackson twisted on his heels without saying another word. He didn't owe Jacob an explanation. This was between BJ and him.

When he caught up to BJ he found her on the phone. He knew it was Teresa on the other end when BJ called her name. On impulse he snatched the phone out of her hand.

"Teresa, stay wherever you are. BJ will be fine here for the night." He ended the call and pocketed the phone.

"You had no right to do that!"

Her eyes blazed with fire, and he could tell she wanted to rake her nails down his face. He couldn't blame her.

"I'm sorry."

She drew back, clearly unprepared for his apology.

He clasped her face between his hands. "I'm sorry," he said again, his voice emphatic.

"Sorry for what, Jackson?" Her tone was scathing. "What are you *really* sorry for?"

"For not telling you the truth sooner."

She tried to pull away, but he held fast. "And what *is* the truth?"

He let out a long, shaky breath. He knew how bad this looked.

"The truth is that I thought I loved Camille once—"

"How could you fall in love with your own brother's wife?" Her expression was incredulous.

"I know what you think. I can see it in your eyes, but it wasn't like that. I met Camille at the same time as Jacob..." A voice inside him told him to tell her the whole truth, but he couldn't. He was on the verge of losing her. He couldn't risk it right now. He would tell her later, when she was calmer. "Jacob and I both fell for her, but Camille fell in love with Jacob and married him. It hurt at the time, but I moved on and then I met you." He caressed her cheek with his thumb. "And almost as soon as I met you, I was completely taken with you."

The harsh sound of her bitter laughter grated on his ears.

"You *thought* you loved Camille, and what? Now you *think* you love me?"

He did love her. He held her tighter. "I do love you," he said softly. This was not exactly how he'd imagined declaring his undying love for her, but that didn't mean his words were any less true.

"No you don't Jackson." She shook her head, her eyes sad. "I'm just a rebound for you. In time you will realise this."

He frowned down at her. "What are you saying?"

"I'm saying that I deserve better than being someone's second choice—"

"You're not my sec—"

"Look, it's over Jackson." This time when she pulled away from him, he let her go.

His eyes narrowed with anger. "So that's it. You're just going to end things and walk away." He took a step towards her. "I told you that I loved you."

He was shouting, and his heart thumped in his chest like a steel drum. He took a deep breath, struggling to rein in his temper. "You love me too. I can see it in your eyes. You're just afraid I'm going to hurt you."

She kept her eyes downcast, refusing to look at him. Anger pumped through his veins along with a sense of helplessness. She couldn't just ignore him and walk away. She couldn't simply up and end things like this.

His hand shot out, and she yelped when he tugged her against him. He glimpsed the barn just a few feet away and he backed her towards it, not stopping until she was trapped between the wooden structure and his body.

"Stop it, Jackson," she protested, struggling against him, but she stopped abruptly when his hands slid down the length of her jean clad legs.

He spun her around, his face buried in the crook of her neck, his hands searching, groping.

"You love me, Bria. Just admit it." He breathed against her neck, and she shivered, her body pulsing with need.

She was stubborn though and refused to say what he already knew. His hands reached around to unfasten her jeans, determined to force her body to reveal what her lips would not.

"Jackson," she rasped when he pushed her jeans, her panties, past her hips leaving her ass bare before him.

He didn't speak as he pulled his hard length from his pants, nudging the tip of his cock against her moist slit.

"You're already wet and I've barely touched you," he whispered against her silky skin. When he pushed forward, deep inside her, stretching her with his length he closed his eyes and groaned, the wet heat of her almost threatening to buckle his knees.

Her gasps of pleasure were soft, feminine and the throaty purrs fuelled his lust until he was thrusting into her with deep, plunging strokes.

"Jackson," she cried out his name, her hips rocking back, her juicy cunt taking the entire pounding length of him.

He held her hips with one hand, while the other reached around to grope her breasts, his hands kneading the soft mounds.

She moaned louder and he felt her desire pulsing through her so strongly. He knew she was close and he quickened his pace, slamming his cock deep inside her, the head of his dick brushing against the mouth of her womb.

He clenched his eyes shut, his jaw tight and pummelled inside her harder, dragging a tortured cry from her lips, her entire body splintering around him as she drenched him with the heat of her climax.

He didn't hold back—couldn't hold back. He buried his ruddy shaft inside her one final time, a harsh grunt tumbling past his lips as he shot his seed to the back of her womb until he was nearly boneless, completely spent.

It was several minutes before he pulled out of her. They righted their clothes in silence, the tension that had been there before, returning once again.

"This doesn't change anything," she said finally, stepping around him.

The hell it didn't. Their lovemaking had been explosive, earth shattering even. Didn't she realise it would never be this good with anyone else?

Headlights flashed in the distance and seconds later a shiny, red convertible pulled up beside them. He cursed under his breath. Fuck. It was Teresa.

He followed after Bria who now marched towards the car. "Bria, don't go like this. We need to talk."

"We're done talking, Jackson. Good night." She slipped into the car and Jackson stood there feeling completely helpless as he watched her pull away and disappear into the darkness.

He stared after the red tail lights until they disappeared in the distance.

"She's a smart girl. She did you a favour." The deep voice, so much like his own, broke through his tumultuous thoughts, startling him.

"A favour?" Rage coursed through his veins as he rounded on Jacob.

"She knows she's a rebound," Jacob said, stepping out of the shadows. "She was smart to end things now before they got complicated. It would have been so much worse for you both had this farce continued."

"Farce?"

"I know this must be hard Jackson, but you don't get over one woman by moving on to another."

Jackson's nostrils flared. His brother was doing what he'd always done—he was trying to take care of him, protect him. Jacob thought he was doing the right thing, but Jackson didn't need protecting—never had.

"I know you mean well, but you don't know what the hell you're talking about." Jacob's eyes widened in surprise when Jackson stood toe to toe with him.

Jackson was the good-natured, easygoing brother. He wasn't often provoked to anger, and he was rarely angry with his brothers, especially Jacob, who he was closest to.

But when it came to Bria, he'd take on the devil himself, if that's what it took to prove the depth of his feelings for her.

"I love her."

"You *think* you love her. Just two months ago you thought you were in love with Camille."

"You're right. I *thought* I was in love with Camille. I cared for her, still do, but what I feel for Bria is real. I know I love her."

He stared his brother in the eye until Jacob was forced to blink. It was a subtle gesture, but it drove his point home.

"You really do love this girl?" Jacob's voice was full of awe.

"Yes. I do." Jackson stepped around him and moved towards the house. "Now I just have to convince Bria."

Chapter Seven

It was Wednesday morning and Jackson couldn't get out of Macon fast enough. He'd tried contacting BJ non-stop, but none of his calls, texts or emails were answered. He needed to get back to Cottonmouth. He needed to see her. He needed to hold her in his arms and look her in the eyes. If he could just do that, he knew he could convince her that his words weren't empty promises.

Jackson slung his suitcase into the back of his car and shut the trunk. He had half his body inside the car when he heard his name. He eased out from behind the wheel and stared up at the woman standing on the porch.

"Camille?" It was barely dawn. What was she doing up so early?

She stepped down from the porch and stopped before him. She seemed nervous and he could tell it was more *for* him than because of him. She still felt guilty—it was written all over her face and he knew what she longed to say.

"It's alright, Camille. You can't help who you fall in love with." He thought of the fiery woman with eyes the colour of a fading sunset in June. She drove him up a wall, but he loved her with his whole heart. "Believe me. I know."

Relief washed over her pretty face, her lips tilting into a small smile. "I never meant to hurt you Jackson."

"I know." He was amazed by how much had changed inside of him over the past few months. When he'd left Macon, he'd been empty and lost, but now—now he felt nothing but peace and it was all because of one woman. He'd told Jacob the truth. He still cared for Camille, he knew he always would. Camille was a special woman and she would always be an important part of his life, but as his sister-in-law, and nothing more.

"I'm happy for you, Jackson. I want you to know that. I can tell you really love this woman." She stood on her tip toes and kissed his cheek. "She's a very lucky girl."

His heart swelled as BJ's face washed before his eyes. "No. I'm the lucky one."

* * * *

"Don't you two have jobs?" BJ slammed the door behind her, her stony gaze wavering between Jeff and Jason. She'd had a long day, and her heart was battered. All she wanted to do was curl up in her bed and pretend that Jackson's scent didn't still linger on her pillow.

The last thing she felt like dealing with was his two look-alike brothers.

"We have jobs." Jason grinned. "But right now our job is guarding you."

"Guarding me?"

"Jackson sent us here to make sure you didn't run away," he added.

She closed her eyes and sighed. "The three of you are morons. This place is my home *and* my job. Where the hell would I go?"

Jeff shrugged. "Not our job to know, just our job to keep you here."

"I'm really starting to believe that Ivy League education was wasted on all of you."

Sexy grins spread across their faces as both of them took a seat on her couch and propped their designer boots on her coffee table.

"Get your feet off my furniture." She glared at them until two sets of boots hit the floor.

"You're spunky, you know that?" Jeff's heartthrob smile was lethal. It had no effect on her, except to remind her of Jackson's dimpled grin. "A real firecracker. It's a shame Jackson won't share you with us."

One eyebrow arched. This was the second time they'd mentioned sharing her. The erotic images that flashed in her head were tempting, but she imagined it was a complicated situation, far more than she was interested in dealing with. Jackson was handful enough anyway. "So it doesn't get weird, sharing each other's women?"

Jason shrugged. "Never was a problem before. It didn't get weird until Camille, but then again that was the first time Jacob was involved. Probably the reason why it got complicated—he has always been possessive."

"*All* of you shared Camille? At the same time?" She gulped. "All of you slept with your brother's wife?"

The look that passed between Jeff and Jason said it all. She shot out of her chair. "What is wrong with all of you?"

"Camille wasn't Jacob's wife at the time."

Her eyes bugged out of her face. She stared at Jeff as if he was an alien. "So!"

"So maybe Jackson should explain the entire situation to you," Jeff said slowly, easing to his feet.

He looked like he couldn't get out of there fast enough. Jason looked equally riled and ready to bolt.

They were both in luck. Jackson barrelled through the front door seconds later.

Perfect. Just the man she wanted to talk to.

"So you share all of your women with your brothers, is that it? When's it my turn to be passed around?"

Jackson looked like a deer caught in the headlights. "You told her," he said to his brothers who only shrugged in response. They were smart men after all.

"Yes they told me. They told me you shared Camille. They told me you've shared other women." She was raising her voice, but she couldn't help it. With Jackson there was always something else, some little detail he neglected to tell her. "So, when's it my turn?"

His eyes narrowed. "You don't get a turn."

"Why not? Every other girl seems to get a turn on the Downing merry-go-round. Why not me?"

"Because I can't share you."

"Why not?"

He shoved a hand through his hair. "Because I love you. I don't want to see you with my brothers."

"You loved Camille. Didn't stop you then."

A muscle twitched in his jaw. "I never loved Camille. I told you that."

She snorted. "Yeah, and you don't love me either."

"Bria—"

"I kind of like the idea of being with you and your brothers." She glanced at Jeff and Jason, who both wore pensive expressions. When Jeff shook his head, his eyes warning her not to say more, she turned back to Jackson. She was too angry to heed any warnings. "A bit kinky, but I think it would be fun."

Jackson's eyes grew cloudy and she hated that she couldn't read him. "Is that what you want?" He asked in a low voice.

She shrugged. "Don't know. Never had the opportunity before. It definitely intrigues me."

"But is it something that you want to do? Would it please you, Bria? Would it make you happy to fuck Jason and Jeff while I watched? Would you enjoy being made love to by the three of us? Or would you only be doing it to hurt me?"

She froze at the tortured sound of his voice. She knew the answers to his questions and she hated herself when she faced the truth. She didn't want any other man but Jackson. The only reason why she would even do it would be to hurt him—and it *would* hurt him. The pain in his eyes tore at her heart. He loved her enough to put aside his feelings in order to make her happy, to please her, but she knew it would kill him to share her.

"You know what? We're just going to excuse ourselves."

She'd forgotten all about Jason and Jeff. Her eyes never left Jackson and his eyes never left hers. She didn't even notice the front door closing shut behind them.

"You're not a rebound," Jackson said, closing the distance between them. "You're not just any woman to me, Bria." He cupped her face. "I love you and it would destroy me to watch you with my brothers, knowing that the only reason why you're with them is because you want to hurt me."

"I know," she said softly, lifting her hand to caress his stumbled jaw. "Which is why I would never do it. I don't want any other man besides you anyway." She loved him with everything inside her. She would never want to do anything to hurt him. Her heart burst with emotion, the words she'd kept locked inside her because she'd been too afraid to risk getting hurt now spilled from her lips. "I love you, Jackson. I—"

He crushed his lips to hers, swallowing up her next words. With his mouth fused to hers, she forgot what she was going to say anyway. She clasped her hands behind his neck, her hands tangling in his hair.

Their tongues duelled, the heated urgency of their kiss causing her to grow hot all over.

He lifted his head, abruptly ending their kiss and cradled her face between his palms.

"I love you, Bria. I just want there to be no doubt in your mind that you are the *only* woman in my heart, and you always will be."

Moisture gathered in her eyes. She hadn't cried in years. Damn Jackson Downing for making her all weepy. "I know," she said with a watery smile. "Now, shut up and kiss me."

He didn't hesitate. He leant forward and in one smooth movement, he covered her mouth with his own, tasting her, claiming her. She encircled his neck, kissing him with her entire body.

Their kiss was heated—urgent—but their hands were slow, their moments measured as they gently skimmed over every intimate inch of their bodies.

His hands settled at her waist, gently prying her shirt from her jeans.

"Mmmm," she moaned when his fingernails lightly scraped against the sensitive skin of her bare belly, causing sharp tingles to fan out across her entire body.

"You like that?" He chuckled against her ear, his warm breath causing tiny goose-bumps to break out along her neck. She shivered in his arms, her pussy growing wet, her entire body throbbing with need.

He manoeuvred her around the coffee table towards the couch until her knees touched the back and her legs buckled. She gasped when her butt settled on the cushion and she realised what he was about to do.

"Jackson, we can't." She shook her head, swatting at his hands that had already unbuttoned her jeans and were now working on the zipper.

He was bent on his knees before her, and he gave her a wolfish grin from between her spread legs as he slowly worked her jeans down the length of her body.

"Why can't we?" He asked, after tossing her jeans to the floor.

She blinked, trying to fight the lust induced fog clouding her brain. "B—because your brothers could walk back here at any moment."

He leant over her, his fingers hooking beneath the elastic of her panties to wrench them off. "They won't."

She started to ask, *how can you be so sure*, but in the next moment he lowered his head and settled his lips against her aching clit. She tunnelled her fingers through his hair, sending it spiking in several directions.

Heat and desire washed over her and her womb contracted with need, her juices spilling from her pussy. She lifted her head to stare at him, her breath catching in her chest when their eyes met. He held her gaze, a wicked twinkle in his cerulean eyes as he slid his tongue through her slit.

It was as if she was in a trance, she couldn't look away. Her entire body vibrated and pulsed with the urge to climax, the need to have Jackson inside her, stretching her, filling her with his hot cum. She tugged at his hair harder, her legs trembling as he sucked on her clit. His fingers probed inside her, pushing past the clenching muscles of her pussy to stroke deep inside her. When he curved his fingers upward, brushing against her g-spot, she arched off the couch, her head flung back and her eyes shut, screaming his name.

"Look at me," he growled against her cunt, and she snapped her gaze to his face, nearly drowning in his clear blue gaze. A rush of warmth started at the apex of her thighs and climbed higher until her cheeks were flushed with heat.

BJ couldn't tear her eyes away from him, the thrusting of his fingers inside her as he watched her while he devoured her pussy, drove her to the brink of climax. She trembled against him, her hips rocking gently as her orgasm began to peak within her. She fought the urge to look away—she was powerless to the onslaught of pleasure that claimed her.

Her thighs clamped around his head at the same time she clenched her eyes shut and cried out his name.

"Mmmmm," he moaned against her pussy, lapping up her juices as violent tremors racked her entire body. Her fingers gripped his head tighter, holding him firmly as she rode his face until she was spent, her body drained. Her breathing was shallow, sweat dotted her skin, and she settled back against the couch completely satiated.

She smiled as Jackson kissed a trail along her body, until his lips once again met hers. He pushed his tongue inside her, gifting her with the tangy taste of her own climax.

"We're not going to fit on the couch together." He said as soon as he lifted his head. In one smooth motion, he pushed aside the coffee table and she let out a small cry when he tugged her to the floor and covered her with his large frame.

"Much better," he said with a naughty smile.

She returned his wicked grin with one of her own, her hands skimming across his shoulders, before sliding towards his torso to undo his shirt.

"I'm half naked, but you're still fully clothed." She pushed his shirt off his body, and waited while he threw it aside. "Much better," she said, repeating his words.

Their lips met again, and like before their hands roamed wildly. The rest of their clothes came off in a blur until they were pressed against each other, skin to naked skin.

Somehow in their tussle of removing clothing she wound up on top. She stroked her hands across his bare chest, enjoying the slide of her fingers through the smattering of hair along his muscled torso.

Jackson groaned her name, his hands clutching her thighs when she bent to capture one of his flat nipples. She swirled her tongue around the hardened peak of one, before moving on to the other, smiling against his skin when he let out a low hiss.

She kissed her way across his chest, along each shoulder, before settling at the base of his throat. She slid her tongue across his salty skin, the taste of him bursting on her tongue.

He gripped her thighs tighter, his nails digging into her soft flesh.

"Bria," he groaned out on a hoarse pant, his chest rising and falling faster than when she'd begun her intimate exploration.

She sat up, her eyes twinkling as she stared down at his flushed face.

"You called my name. Was there something you wanted?" She asked innocently.

His eyes darkened with lust, and she knew the time for playing was about to come to a swift end.

"I need you to get on him."

She twisted around, her cunt clenching tighter when she glimpsed the hard rod of his cock jutting towards the sky.

"You mean that?" She asked with a mischievous smile.

"Bria," he growled, his hands moving to her hips. "Ride me."

His voice was thick with lust and desire and the gravely sound wrapped around her, causing her nipples to tighten.

Fresh juice filled her sheath, and when she slid back along his belly, she left a wet trail.

She angled herself just above the tip of his cock, holding herself still as she held his gaze. Their gazes clashed, neither one able to look away as she slowly lowered herself onto his engorged shaft.

She moaned out his name, and it mingled with his own tortured groan as she took him inside her, the thick length of him stretching her, filling her.

When he was pressed to the hilt, she paused before slowly moving her hips, giving her body a moment to adjust. Her cunt poured forth more wet hot juice, making her strokes slick and slippery, and she took him deeper and harder until they both were crying out in pleasure.

"Jackson," she called his name, her hips jerking wildly atop him as her fingers dug into his shoulders.

He took over the rhythm, grasping her waist, rotating her on his cock until tingling sensations once again gathered at the centre of her sex.

He moved her harder and faster, and she dug her nails deeper until a wave of heat surged inside her and she exploded, coming all around him, drenching his cock in her wet heat.

Blinding light flashed behind her closed lids and in the distance she heard the tortured rasp of her name, seconds before Jackson's body stiffened and a rush of warmth filled her pussy. He writhed beneath her, his hands clenching her waist tight until the shudders that claimed his body quieted.

She slumped forward, resting her cheek against his chest, listening to the steady rhythm of his heart beating. He stroked her back and she closed her eyes, feeling safe and cherished in Jackson's strong arms.

"I love you," he murmured against her hair.

She lifted her head and smiled. "I love you too."

She leant down to kiss his lips but stopped when the knob to the front door began to rattle.

She glared at Jackson, and began to scramble around for her clothing but stopped when he gripped her arm.

There was something in his eyes, something dark and provocative, a look she'd never seen before.

The front door opened and Jeff and Jason stumbled in, their eyes wide with surprise. Their shock soon gave way to lust, and it burned in their sapphire gazes, reminding her that she was stark naked.

She moved to cover herself, but Jackson's hand on her arm tightened and she stared at him, her eyes rounding when she realised what he was doing.

"Jackson?"

"If you're not comfortable with this, then we stop now."

She blinked, her mind scrambling to make sense of his words. There was no denying she was curious about the possibility of being made love to by all three of them, but her curiosity was not worth the pain it would cause Jackson.

"But you just said you didn't share."

Jackson smiled down into Bria's lovely face, her eyes confused.

"I don't. Not often. But I'm not against it. "

"But you said..."

He kissed the tip of her nose. "I had to know that you wanted me, and only me. It was important for me to know that you were willing to set aside your desires because you didn't want to hurt me."

Her eyes flashed. "So, it was a test," she snapped, but he wasn't bothered by her irritation. Soon his lovely Bria would forget all about her anger. In a few moments the only thing in her head would be thoughts of the pleasure he and his brothers could give her.

"Not so much as a test, as it was a need to feel secure with you. I had to know that you loved me, wanted only me, that you would be happy with only me." He tangled his hand in her hair then, and tipped her head back. He dipped his head and claimed her lips, his tongue probing her sweet mouth.

Bria wasn't the only one with insecurities. After Camille, he hadn't realised how much he needed to know that the woman he loved wanted only him, that she desired only him. He could share Bria with his brothers, but that was because he knew he had her heart, her complete devotion.

He tugged his lips from hers and stepped away, a smile crossing his face when she whimpered.

Bria groaned in protest when Jackson brought an end to their kiss. She opened her eyes, expecting to meet Jackson's smiling gaze, but instead she saw Jeff standing before her, wearing a roguish smile. She gasped when she felt a hand settle against her hip and turned to see Jason at her back, wearing a handsome smile.

It just didn't seem fair that all of the Downing brothers were wickedly handsome, but she didn't have time to ponder the injustice of such a feat, when Jeff claimed her lips.

Where Jackson's lips were demanding and possessive, Jeff's were coaxing, teasing. She wrapped her arms around his neck, returning the kiss, enjoying the soft flutters of pleasure that danced in her belly.

Jeff broke their kiss and tugged her to the floor, pulling her atop his hard body. He tangled his hand in her hair, once again dragging her lips to his. She lost herself in the wondrous feel of his mouth, the heated pleasure of his kiss.

A soft moan escaped her lips when she felt Jason slide behind her, the tip of his cock nudging against her puckered anus. He didn't push inside, instead he teased her with the tips of his fingers, causing goose-bumps to break out across her heated skin.

She cried out when in one fluid motion Jeff slid her down the length of his body and lifted her hips, tugging her down on his waiting shaft. The invasion was so abrupt, so unexpected, that she fought to accommodate his thick length. Still gripping her hips, he thrust her down on his engorged flesh, her breasts bobbing before him.

Blinding pleasure sliced through her belly and she moaned, the sound hoarse and needy to her own ears. She rocked on Jeff's cock, her orgasm steadily building inside her. She was so close, so close to tumbling over the edge and falling into the wondrous rapture of her climax. But when Jason slipped inside her, his thick cock pushing past the first ring of muscle, she stiffened, her next breath lodging in her chest.

Jason stilled, his warm breath caressing the back of her neck.

"It's all right. Just relax, Bria."

She felt so full, her body stretching to accommodate the girth and length of them both. Her gaze darted around the room, searching for Jackson. When their eyes met she relaxed, as a contented warmth spreading through her at the reassurance in his eyes. That's when she noticed that he sat stretched out in a chair across the room, pumping his dick with his fist as he watched his brothers give her pleasure.

Jason pushed forward then, dragging her attention back to him and Jeff who continued to shove his cock inside her, his face twisted in pleasurable agony.

She fell forward then, bracing her hands against Jeff's shoulders when Jason buried his entire length inside her. Her rectum stretched around him, but the fit was so tight and she felt stuffed, the pressure overwhelming.

She wanted to pull away from him, but Jason held fast, his hand reaching around to strum her clit, building a maelstrom of sensations inside her that left her gasping for air.

"Oh, God," she screamed, her eyes clenched shut, her nails digging into Jeff's shoulders.

She came so quickly, so unexpectedly that she swore her heart skipped a beat. Jeff and Jason plunged inside her on hurried strokes, their cocks going deeper and harder, stretching her, filling her. She cried out at the hot blast of semen against her womb, her eyes flying open and she watched Jeff, his eyes shut tight, his lips parted as he let out a ragged groan.

She'd almost forgotten about Jason, he'd stilled as Jeff came inside her, but now he moved within her, his thrusts driving deeper, his cock filling her up. He panted against her ear, his breaths growing choppy, stilted and when he tensed behind her, his cock twitching inside her anus—she moaned. He exploded within her, his warm seed coating the walls of her rectum—his shout of completion strangled and hoarse rattling the walls.

He slumped against her, his sweat slick chest pressed against her back. She closed her eyes with a contented sigh, but when a hand gripped the back of her head she looked up, her gaze clashing with Jackson.

She didn't say a word, neither of them did, and with his brothers still nestled inside her, she leant forward, her lips parting to take Jackson's cock down her throat.

He held the back of her head tight and groaned, a deep soul stirring sound as she sucked him off, her head bobbing vigorously. She watched him beneath hooded eyes. The muscles in his bare chest were corded with tension, and his veins strained against his bronzed skin. She tightened her lips around him, moving faster, and she moaned around his cock when she felt a tiny bead of cum on her tongue.

"That's it Bria." He breathed. "Suck my cock."

She closed her eyes, taking him all the way to the back of her throat. He let out a strangled groan, his nails digging into her scalp. She cupped his balls, massaging gently and that was his undoing. He shouted out her name as he shoved his length into her mouth as far as it would go and held her head still, his warm cum shooting from his dick to the back of her throat. She worked her mouth, her lips, her throat, swallowing every drop until his balls were empty, his body completely spent.

She was exhausted, utterly satiated and she felt as if she was nothing more than a mass of boneless jelly. In the dark corners of her mind, she was vaguely aware of Jackson lifting her into his arms and carrying her upstairs. By the time he laid her down atop her bed, she was fast asleep.

* * * *

Jackson rushed into the house, his entire body vibrating with excitement.

"Bria! Bria!" He screamed at the top of his lungs.

She burst through the kitchen door, her eyes filled with concern. "Jackson, what is it?"

He pulled her into his arms and hoisted her into the air.

She gripped his shoulders. "Okay, you're really starting to scare me. What's going on?"

He set her back down, but not before he planted a long, hard kiss against her pretty lips.

He forced himself to drag his mouth from hers, a small grin curving at the edges of his lips at the desire that burned in her gaze. There would be plenty of time for that later, *after* he told her the good news.

He pulled out the map from his back pocket and spread it across the coffee table. Three large red "X's" marked the map and he pointed to each of them.

"You did it, babe."

She looked at him, puzzled. "Did what?"

"You know how we started drilling a few days ago?"

Her eyes lit up. "You found oil?"

He nodded. "In all three spots. You were right on."

Her scream pierced his ears, but he didn't care. He swung her around in his arms, and they laughed like two little kids.

"You're going to be a rich woman," he said when he finally put her down again.

"And you're going to be a rich man. No correction. A *richer* man."

Her words sobered him instantly. He'd been waiting for the perfect moment, the perfect time to ask her. His heart thumped so loudly, he could barely hear anything else.

"Speaking of riches, that reminds me." He set her down, his hands shaking slightly. "My brothers and I have always been driven to make more money, acquire more land and honestly that all used to be important to me too." He fished inside his pocket as he went down on one knee. "Until I met you." He held out a piece of paper and nodded for her to take it.

"Jackson what are you doing?" She asked in a shaky voice.

"Just read it."

She skimmed it, the paper rattling in her trembling hand. "Jackson, you don't have to do this," she said when she was done.

"You're wrong. I do. Cottonmouth belongs to you and it belongs in your family, which is why I had the deed to the land put in your name. It's my wedding present to you. But whether you marry me or not I still want you to have what is rightfully yours."

"Marry you? Wedding pre—" Her eyes widened. She must have forgotten he was still down on bended knee, but comprehension dawned in her gaze when her eyes landed on the ring in his hand.

"Jackson?"

"Bria Jaslene Parker. Will you marry me?"

Epilogue

The bride was radiant in a bone white Vera Wang gown, a gown that BJ would have probably burned had Teresa not kept it locked up at her home under watch and key until their wedding day.

"You are stunning." Jackson beamed down at his wife who floated around the dance floor in his arms.

She smiled up at him, her eyes alight with love. "How long do I have before I get to take this off?"

He rolled his eyes. "You're such a romantic. How did I get so lucky?"

"I'm still trying to figure that out."

She laughed then, and it was infectious. He pulled her in tighter, holding her close to his body.

"I love you, Bria," he whispered against her ear, his heart bursting each and every time he said the words. He may have been joking, but he really couldn't believe how lucky he was. He'd met her at a time when he'd been at his lowest and full of doubts. Nothing about them, or their initial meeting would have suggested love, but they'd found it.

He held her closer, his heart beating in time with hers. He counted himself among the luckiest men in the world that BJ now held his heart, and he held hers. She was loyal to those she loved and was as tough as any woman he'd ever met, but deep down—when they were alone and it was just them—she opened up to him, and showed him a vulnerable woman who sought love and reassurance just as eagerly as anyone. She was the other half of his heart, his soul, and when he looked into her eyes, he saw a future filled with little girls with golden eyes and plenty of sass and little boys full of the Downing charm.

She stopped on the dance floor and wrapped her arms around his neck, pulling him close.

"I love you too, Jackson Downing," she said in a quiet voice before stealing a quick kiss. When he lifted his head, her eyes were glowing with mischief.

"Now can we get out of here? I'm ready to start our honeymoon."

"Bria." He shook his head, but she was already pulling him off the dance floor and away from the crowd of guests. He glanced back. No one seemed to notice they were making a getaway.

"Bria, I think we—"

"Shhh." She placed a delicate finger against his lips. "It's our wedding night. What can they really say?"

She had a good point. He relented as he let her drag him away.

* * * *

"I cannot believe them." Teresa fumed as she stomped off in the direction BJ and Jackson had disappeared. She knew exactly where they were headed. This had to be all

BJ's doing. She was going to ruin that gown if it was the last thing she did. Teresa was livid. Didn't BJ know how many strings she'd had to pull to get a Vera Wang wedding gown at the last minute?

She was halfway across the dance floor when a hand snaked around her waist.

"What the—" She found herself clinging to a set of broad shoulders until she realised who they belonged to, and dropped her hands.

"Let them go. It's their wedding night," Jeff said in a husky voice, his warm breath laced with alcohol, fanning her face. Her nipples tightened and she had to bite her lip to keep from letting out a moan. What was it with this man that sent her body into overdrive?

"You're drunk," she said in a flat voice, trying to twist out of his arms.

His eyes lit up. "Not *that* drunk. Except for driving, I can still perform any necessary duties required of me."

She glared at him. "Are you always such a gentleman?"

The intended insult had no effect on him as he held her even closer. "What can I say? I love the ladies."

"And the ladies love you, no doubt." She snorted. "You're a real charmer, a class act. I am going to shed some serious tears tonight thinking about how I missed out on ... " She looked him up and down, "...*this.*" She pushed at his chest. "Let go of me."

He chuckled and then leant into her, his mouth nuzzling the crook of her neck. Despite her scathing words, she couldn't deny he turned her on and she had to fight the urge to shudder against him when her pussy clenched.

"I don't know why you keep fighting me, why you keep fighting *this* every time I see you. I can feel your nipples against my chest and I know if I slide my fingers under this teeny tiny skirt of yours, I'll find your tight pussy dripping wet. Stop trying to deny it, Teresa. I know you want me. I don't know why you keep letting our age difference stop you. It's only eight years anyway, which is nothing when you think about it."

Fury exploded inside her and she pushed at him until he was forced to release her. He had no right to talk to her like she was one of his cheap playthings.

"Look around Jeff. They're dozens of women here. If you want someone to fuck go grab one of them."

He inched closer, his blue eyes flashing a stormy grey. "But I don't want them. I want you."

"But I don't want *you*."

"You're lying."

She was in many ways, but there was a part of her that didn't want him, at least not what he was offering.

"I feel sorry for you." That got his attention as one brow peaked. "You'll never have what your older brothers have, you'll never find a woman who wants more from you than your money, great sex and a bit of fun with a good looking man. Maybe it's because you're immature or maybe you just don't want something of substance, something real. But it's a shame because I know deep down you're a good guy who's just pretending to be a dick."

She twisted on her heels and started to walk away, but stopped to glance at him from over her shoulder. His eyes were clouded over and she almost regretted her harsh words, until his lips curved into a cocky grin.

She shook her head. "You know what, Jeff? You were right about one thing. I was lying. I do want you, but I also want more, which is something you just don't have in you to give me."

She spun around and walked off, trying to be certain if she'd really seen determination flash in his gaze. She shook her head. It didn't matter if she had. Jeff Downing was the quintessential playboy. The only thing he was determined to get was into her pants.

* * * *

BJ stretched her arms above her head and yawned. "We should probably get back now before they send out a search party."

"Now you want to get back. *Now* you care if anyone's worried about us."

"You're right. We should just stay." She flopped back down to rest her head atop his chest and snuggled against him, a smile curling her lips when he chuckled.

"I agree. We should get back, but I don't think I could move now even if I wanted to. Someone had her wicked way with me and wore me out."

She lifted her head again, her hair falling over one shoulder to brush his chest. "It's our wedding night. What can I say? I was impatient."

"Apparently too impatient to wait until we could make it back to a bed. What is it with you and barns?"

"Not any barn." Her eyes darted around the dark space, the fading sunlight bathing the area in a tawny glow. "This is where we first made love."

"I know." His voice was low, but his eyes blazed with the intensity of his love.

She gazed into Jackson's face, her throat clogging with such a deep emotion that she couldn't speak. It had been that way when she'd struggled to say her vows. Everyone thought she was having cold feet. Only Jackson knew she was simply too overwhelmed by the moment to speak, a lot like right now.

She stroked her hand down his cheek. His eyes were closed and she knew he was beginning to drift off to sleep.

"I love you," she said quietly, gently kissing his lips before once again laying her head atop his chest. She'd never imagined that there was a piece of her missing until she'd met Jackson. But now she felt whole, her heart overflowing with love for him.

She listened to the sound of his even heartbeat and gazed up into the sky until her eyelids grew heavy and she fell asleep wrapped in the arms of the man she would love forever.

About the Author

Nadia Aidan lives, works and writes on the West Coast in the United States. Under her real name, Nadia holds a PhD in Political Science and Public Policy and by day she works as an Assistant Professor.

She is the self proclaimed new face of interracial and multicultural erotic romance and writes across all genres, from historical, to fantasy/sci-fi to contemporary. In addition to writing erotic romances Nadia enjoys reading other authors, playing flag football, studying muay thai, working out, listening to music, scuba diving, and target shooting.

Her other interests include collecting Top Cow comics, especially Witchblade and Tomb Raider. She loves professional football and soccer. Her favourite teams are the Washington Redskins and Manchester United, respectively.

Nadia loves watching, reading about, and writing about strong, assertive heroines which is why she is an enduring fan of Fight Girls, Xena, Buffy, American Gladiators—New and Old, and La Femme Nikita!

Nadia Aidan loves to hear from readers. You can find her contact information, website details and author profile page at http://www.total-e-bound.com.

Total-E-Bound Publishing

www.total-e-bound.com

Take a look at our exciting range of literagasmic™
erotic romance titles and discover pure quality
at Total-E-Bound.